WILLIAM

AT WAR

Richmal Crompton was born in Lancashire in 1890. The first story about William Brown appeared in *Home* magazine in 1919, and the first collection of William stories was published in book form three years later. In all, thirty-eight William books were published, the last one in 1970, after Richmal Crompton's death.

'Probably the funniest, toughest children's books ever written'
Sunday Times on the Just William series

'Richmal Crompton's creation [has] been famed for his cavalier attitude to life and those who would seek to circumscribe his enjoyment of it ever since he first appeared'
Guardian

WILLIAM

AT WAR

RICHMAL CROMPTON

FOREWORD BY JOHN SESSIONS

ILLUSTRATED BY THOMAS HENRY

MACMILLAN CHILDREN'S BOOKS

This selection first published 1995 by Macmillan Children's Books

This edition published 2011 by Macmillan Children's Books
a division of Macmillan Publishers Limited
20 New Wharf Road, London N1 9RR
Basingstoke and Oxford
Associated companies throughout the world
www.panmacmillan.com

ISBN 978-0-330-54520-4

1 3 5 7 9 8 6 4 2

A CIP catalogue record for this book is available from
the British Library.

Printed and bound by CPI Group (UK) Ltd, Croydon CR0 4YY

CONTENTS

FOREWORD

Life today. We all know sunny streets on perfect Saturday or Sunday afternoons, with lawnmowers growling and dads washing cars. How much the streets have changed since William's day. So much more noise. Or so much more silence perhaps, with children glued enraptured to their iPhones instead of jumping from puddle to puddle and getting gloriously filthy.

William Brown's world somehow always seems to be sunny, although of course there are wet days too. How else would William and the Outlaws have puddles to splash about in to splatter themselves with mud? And everything is different in William's world . . . how old the cars look and how few there were on the roads compared to today. And then there are all the grown-ups who seem to have been sent into Williamland only to be tormented by the Outlaws. What a peculiar lot they are. Adults forever banished from the joyous feeling of being eleven, from holding up a jam-jar full of tadpoles and watching the sunshine sparkle through it. Did the women really swan about with half a dozen fox furs wrapped around their necks? Yes, they did. Did permanently furious colonels really screw a single eyeglass into one of their furious eyes? Yet again, they did. Richmal Crompton saw nothing wrong with this. Hers is a world of best foot forward, of bracingly cold baths, a world of no-nonsense.

Richmal's world was also one where children should be seen and not heard, do as they're told and not get upset if they're ignored or thought of as a 'bad lot'. But William and his friends, especially Violet Elizabeth Bott, have many ways of getting round the irksome little problem of being ignored. Ahh, Violet Elizabeth Bott. She should be the patron saint of all girls who confuse and irritate boys. There is really something rather magnificent about her. I hope you agree.

I have one particular favourite story about

William. It's the one when the tall, lanky French boy comes to stay with the Browns in order to improve his wobbly English. Today it's rightly considered rather naff to laugh at foreigners because of their strong accents and difficulty with finding the right words. But when Richmal Crompton was writing, eighty and ninety years ago (at the time that Britain thought it was the centre of the universe), it was considered perfectly natural to regard all foreigners as ludicrous. However, she manages to make this French boy charming and vulnerable while also being screamingly funny. I don't know why I like this story the best. Perhaps it's because William creates so much chaos among the adults. They pant and gibber and try their best to hang on to their sanity. They only just manage it.

I hope you enjoy reading William as much as I did when I was young. When I was young. Hmmm. Now that really is a horribly long time ago . . .

John Sessions

CHAPTER I

WILLIAM AND A.R.P.

'WELL, I don' see why we shun't have one, too,' said William morosely. 'Grown-ups get all the fun.'

'They *say* it's not fun,' said Ginger.

'Yes, they say that jus' to put us off,' said William. 'I bet it *is* fun all right. I bet it'd be fun if *we* had one, anyway.'

'Why don't we have one?'

'I asked 'em that. I said, "Why can't we have one?" an' they said, "Course you can't. Don't be so silly." Silly! S'not *us* what's silly, an' I told 'em so. I bet we could do it as well as what they do. Better, come to that. Yes, I bet that's what they're frightened of – us doin' it better than what they do.'

'What do they do, anyway?' demanded Douglas.

'They have a jolly good time,' said William vaguely. 'Smellin' gases an' bandagin' each other an' tryin' on their gas masks. I bet they bounce out at each other in their gas masks, givin' each other frights. I've thought of lots of games you could play with gas masks, but no one'll let me try. They keep mine locked up. Lot of good it'll be in a war locked up where I can't get at it. Huh!'

There was a pause, during which the Outlaws silently contemplated the absurdity of this situation.

'I told 'em I ought to be able to wear it a bit each day jus' for practice,' went on William. 'I told 'em I wouldn't be much use in a war 'less I did. Why, anyone'd think they *wanted* me to get killed, keepin' my gas mask where I can't get at it. It's same as murder. Just 'cause of us playin' gladiators in 'em the first day we got 'em! Well, the bit of damage it did was easy to put right. It was a jolly good thing really, 'cause it sort of showed where it was weak. They said I'd been *rough* on it. Well, if war's not s'posed to be *rough* I don't know what is. Seems cracked to me to have somethin' for a war you can't be *rough* in. I bet they're rough in 'em in those ole classes they go to.'

'Well, even if they won't let us go to theirs,' said Ginger, 'I don't see they could stop us havin' one of our own.'

'No, that's a jolly good idea,' said William, brightening. 'A jolly good idea. They can't stop us doin' that.'

'We'll call it A.R.P. Junior Branch,' suggested Ginger. 'Same as what they do with Conservative Clubs an' things.'

'Yes,' agreed William. 'A.R.P. Junior Branch. An' we'll do the same things they do an' do 'em a jolly sight better.

I bet they'll be jolly grateful to us when a war comes along. I bet we'll save the country while they're messin' about tryin' to remember where they put their gas masks. If they won't let me have mine, I'll make one. I bet they're quite easy to make. Jus' a bit of ole mackintosh cut round for a face an' a sort of tin with holes to breathe through. I've got an ole mackintosh an' the tin I keep my caterpillars in'd do to breathe through. It's got holes in ready, an' I bet, if caterpillars can breathe through it, I can. Only two of 'em've died.'

William and Ginger canvassed the junior inhabitants of the village that evening, and Henry and Douglas wrote out the notice and prepared the old barn for the meeting. The preparation of the old barn was not difficult. It consisted simply of an ancient packing case for William's use as lecturer and demonstrator. The audience was expected to sit on the floor. The audience generally did sit on the floor. It grumbled, but it put up with it. The notice was the work of Ginger alone. It was executed in blacking ('borrowed' from the kitchen) on a piece of cardboard broken from the box in which his mother kept her best hat. It ran:

AIR RADE PRECORSHUN
JUNIER BRANCH
ENTRUNCE FRE.

'They'll come if it's free,' said Douglas, with a tinge of bitterness in his voice. 'They always come to free things.'

'They'll jolly well have to come,' said William sternly. 'What'll they do in a war if they don't know how to do it? They've gotter learn same as grown-ups. I bet they'll feel jolly silly, the grown-ups, when this war comes along an' we do it all a jolly sight better than what they do. P'raps they won't put on such a lot of swank after *that*. I bet they *knew* we'd do it better than them, an' that's why they've been tryin' to keep us out of it. Huh!'

At the time advertised for the meeting, a thin stream of children began to trickle over the fields to the old barn. There were Victor Jameson and Ronald Bell – always friends and supporters of the Outlaws – Arabella Simpkins, a red-haired, sharp-featured maiden of domineering disposition, dragging after her a small sister exactly like her, and a rag, tag, and bob-tail of juveniles. With much scuffling and shouting and criticising of the accommodation provided, they settled themselves on the floor. William's mounting upon the packing case was the signal for cheers that increased in volume as the rotten wood gave way and he disappeared backwards. He picked himself up with a not very successful attempt at dignity, smoothed back his hair, collected the scattered sheaves of his lecture notes, scowled round upon his audience, and,

putting several bits of broken wood together for a plat-
form, took his stand on it precariously.

'Ladies an' gentl'men,' he shouted above the uproar,
which was still far from subsiding, 'will you kindly shut up
an' listen to me? I'm goin' to tell you how to win the war.
Well, d'you want to win the war, or *don't* you . . . Arabella
Simpkins, shut up makin' all that noise . . . Victor Jameson, I tell you I'm tellin' you how to win the war . . . You'll
be sorry you've not listened when it comes an' you're all
blown to bits. You've gotter listen to me, if you want to
win the war. D'you want to be blown to bits by bombs an'
balloons an' things jus' 'cause you wouldn't shut up an'
listen to me? . . . I *didn't* start her howling. She started herself . . . Well, I only said she'd be blown to bits if she didn't
listen. I *never* said I'd blow her to bits . . . All right, *tell*
your mother. I don't care . . . All right, *take* her home an'
I'm jolly glad you're goin' . . . Shut *up,* all of you!'

After the departure of Arabella Simpkins with her
small sister – the small sister still howling, and Arabella
still threatening reprisals – the uproar subsided slightly,
and William, purple-faced and hoarse with shouting,
turned to his typewritten papers. They were the notes of
Ethel's A.R.P. classes, which he had managed to abstract
from her writing desk, and he had not had time to look
through them before the lecture.

'LADIES AN' GENTL'MEN,' HE SHOUTED ABOVE THE UPROAR,
'WILL YOU KINDLY SHUT UP AN' LISTEN TO ME? I'M GOIN'
TO TELL YOU HOW TO WIN THE WAR.'

'Now, listen,' he said, 'an' I'll tell you all about these
gases an' suchlike. They're' – he studied his notes with
frowning concentration – 'per-sis-tent! That's what they are.

6

Per-sis-tent. Well, that's what it says here. It *mus'* be right, mus'n't it, if it says so here? An' there's one – well, it's got a long name, I won't say it to you 'cause you can't understand it, an' it smells like pear drops. It *says* so, I tell you. Shut up . . . No, I've not got any pear drops. I never said I'd got any pear drops. Why don't you *listen* when I'm givin' a lecture? I wouldn't give you any if I had, either, not with you not giving me any of your liquorice all-sorts last Sat'day. You *had* got some. You were eatin' 'em. Shut *up* about pear drops. I never said a bomb was made of pear drops. I said it *smelt* of 'em . . . Well,' uncertainly, 'p'raps it is. P'raps it is made of pear drops. No, it doesn't say so here . . . Well, so are you, anyway . . . I didn't. I said the bombs *smelt* of 'em . . . It says so here . . . I dunno . . . All right, if you don't want to listen, *don't*. I don't care . . . No, I've not gotter bomb. Shut up about pear drops. I'm sick of 'em. I'm not talking about pear drops. I'm tellin' you how to win the war . . . Well, you gotter know what bombs smell like to win a war, haven't you? I *do* know what I'm talkin' about . . . I never said they dropped pear drops. I said they dropped bombs. I said these bombs smelt of pear drops . . . I *dunno* why they smell of pear drops . . . Listen,' he pleaded, hastily scanning his paper, 'I'll tell you somethin' else if you'll listen . . .'

But the meeting was breaking up in disorder. Its members had seized on the subject of pear drops and refused to be diverted from it. In any case, they wanted to do something a little more exciting than sit and listen to William holding forth from a typewritten paper. William was not altogether sorry for the curtailment of his lecture. He had caught a glimpse of several lengthy and quite unintelligible words further down on the sheet and was glad to be rescued from them.

'All right,' he said. 'We'll do bandagin' next. We've got some bandagin' things.'

Several members of his audience, however, refused to stay.

'Said he was goin' to tell us how to win the war, an' all he could do was talk about *pear drops*,' they said indignantly. '*Pear drops*. Tellin' us what *pear drops* smell like. I bet we know what *pear drops* smell like all right without *him* tellin' us. Batty. That's what he is.'

They lingered only to exchange a brisk volley of insults with the Outlaws, ending on both sides when further invention failed with 'Pear drop yourself!' then took their way over the field to the village to resume the normal activities of their life.

'*Now*,' said William, addressing his depleted audience, 'we've gotter practise bandagin'. That's what *they* do. Then, when people get blown up by these pear – I mean bombs – you can bandage 'em up . . . Where's the bandagin' things, Henry?'

Henry, with an air of modest pride, brought out a cardboard dress-box full of a strange assortment of ribbons, straps, bits of material, with a few genuine bandages somewhat grimy and blood-stained. Henry's mother was what is known as a 'hoarder', and Henry had carefully gone through the cardboard boxes of odds and ends that she kept in the spare bedroom and taken out everything that could possibly, by any stretch of the imagination, figure as a 'bandage'. He assuaged his conscience (for Henry was a conscientious boy) by the reflection that they had been put there in case they should ever 'come in useful', and that that contingency had now arrived. The real bandages he had acquired the evening before by an act of stupendous heroism – deliberately drawing blood by means of a blunt penknife on both legs and an arm.

'Gracious, child!' his mother had said. 'What on *earth* have you been doing?'

'I – sort of slipped against somethin',' said Henry vaguely.

His mother was fortunately a generous bandager, and Henry had thus acquired three bandages of enormous length that, cut into smaller portions, made a brave show.

'Now,' ordered William, 'one of every two's gotter have a bandage an' bandage the other. Then do it the other way round. That's what we've gotter do now. Practise bandagin' each other up for when we get blown to pieces by these pear – these bombs. Let's start on each other's heads an' work down to each other's feet. That's the way they do it. We've gotter work very hard with this. All these bits of stuff an' ribbons an' things'll do jus' as well as real bandages. Jus' to practise on. Now we'll start on heads. Have you all got

10

somethin' to bandage with? Well, start when I say "go" an' see who can finish first. One . . . two . . . three . . . *Go!*'

The free fight that ensued was, perhaps, only to be expected. Each pair was scuffling for the possession of the bandage even before the signal for the bandage race was given. The bandaging of heads degenerated almost at once into the punching of heads. Bandages were used as weapons to trip up, to gag, to tie up, to flick, and generally to obstruct, harass and annoy. Old scores were wiped off, new scores were accumulated – all in a gloriously carefree spirit of give and take. The barn was full of joyously shouting, scuffling, fighting boys.

At first William tried to quell the uproar.

'*Stop* it,' he shouted sternly. 'Stop it an' get on bandagin'. It's a *bandagin'* class, I tell you, not a wild-beast fight. Don't you want to *learn* to bandage each other when these pear—?'

At this moment Victor Jameson lassoed him from behind with a piece of black velvet that had formed the belt of Henry's mother's last year's evening dress, and he went crashing to the ground. After that he forgot about the bandaging and joined heartily in the fight, shouting encouragement and defiance to everyone round him indiscriminately. It wasn't till the bandages were reduced to shreds that they stopped, breathless and exhilarated, and surveyed the battlefield. Bits of material were in their hair and eyes and noses and all over their clothes. They looked like the survivors of a remnant sale . . .

'I got you in a jolly good one,' panted William to Ginger.

'Yes,' said Ginger, 'an' I got you a jolly good one back.'

'You went with a jolly fine wallop when I tripped you up,' panted Victor Jameson.

'Yes, an' I'd've tied you up if the bandage hadn't broke. I'd got it right round your legs.'

A small boy near the door was howling loudly and asserting that someone had pinched his bandage and stuck their finger in his eye.

'I'm goin' home,' he bawled. 'I'm not learnin' to win no more wars. It's nothin' but people talkin' about pear drops, an' pinchin' your bandage, an' stickin' their fingers in your eyes . . . It's not fair . . . I'm goin' to tell my mother.'

'All right,' said William. 'Go home. We don't want you. That's the end of the bandagin' class, anyway.'

The small boy departed still howling, followed by one or two others who had fared badly in the bandage fight.

Though still further depleted in numbers, the temperature of the A.R.P. class was now considerably raised. Its members were ready and eager for the next adventure.

'Come on,' said Ginger gleefully. 'What do we do next?'

William looked a little doubtful.

'Well, they practise wearin' their gas masks,' he said, 'but we can't do that 'cause we've not got 'em. I tried makin' one with a bit of ole mackintosh an' a tin, but the tin wouldn't stay in the hole.'

A faint anxiety clouded his spirit at the memory. It had certainly been an old mackintosh, but he wasn't really sure that it was old enough to be cut up into a gas mask. He had hung it in the hall so that the hole did not show, but his mother was certain to discover it sooner or later. She might even be discovering it at that moment . . . But the exhilaration of the bandage fight still remained, and he decided not to waste the glorious present in anticipating trouble.

'We only want things over our faces,' Ronald Bell was saying. 'Anythin' over our faces'd do for gas masks.'

Henry had a sudden inspiration.

'Flower pots!' he yelled excitedly. 'Flower pots! We've got some big 'uns. Come on!'

Whooping, shouting, leaping, they ran across the field, down the road, to Henry's home.

'Come in at the back garden,' said Henry. 'They're by the greenhouse. An' this is the day the ole gard'ner doesn't come. Don't make a noise.'

They entered the garden gate in single file and looked warily around them. The garden was empty. No one was

13

in sight. By the greenhouse stood piles of large red flower pots, in which the gardener meant to pot his chrysanthemums the next morning. Henry tried one on. It completely enveloped his face.

His voice came muffled, but joyous, from behind it. 'Come on. Put 'em on. They make jolly fine gas masks.'

Hilariously the band put the flower pots over their heads and began to leap about in wild excitement. They did not intend to do anything beyond leaping about, but the spirit of the bandage fight still lingered with them, and they were soon charging each other with re-echoing war whoops, putting on new flower pots as the old ones were shattered. They went on till no new flower pots were left, and the place was littered with fragments of pottery. Then they stopped and looked at each other in growing dismay.

Henry glanced apprehensively towards the house.

'Gosh!' he said. 'It's a good thing my mother's out, an' Cook puts on the wireless loud 'cause she's deaf. Let's get away quick.'

They hurried from the scene of the crime as fast as they could.

'P'raps they'll think it was an aeroplane accident or somethin',' said Ginger hopefully.

'An' p'raps they won't,' said Henry. 'More like they'll

14

start on me straight away without even givin' me a chance to explain, same as they always do.'

'Tell 'em we were only havin' gas-mask drill,' said William. 'Tell 'em it was their fault for keepin' our gas masks locked up.'

'Yes,' said Henry sarcastically. 'Yes, that'll do a lot of good, won't it?'

A few of the more fearful spirits at this point decided that they had had enough A.R.P. practice for one day and set off homewards (by a miracle the casualties of the flower-pot fight consisted of nothing more than a few scratches), but the Outlaws, with Ronald Bell and Victor Jameson and a few other brave spirits, felt this to be a tame ending. The exhilaration of the two fights had produced a spirit of dare-devil recklessness. They were all going to get into trouble, anyway, over Henry's flower pots, and they might as well, they felt, be killed for the proverbial sheep.

'Come on,' said Ginger. 'Let's do somethin' else. What else do they do?'

William considered.

'Well,' he said, 'there *was* somethin' else. I saw it in Robert's book. It was called a jolly long name – somethin' beginnin' with De. Detramination, or somethin'. It was takin' all your clothes off an' havin' a hose pipe turned on you.'

15

'Come on!' they shouted with whoops of joy. 'Come on!'

'Come to my house,' yelled Ginger. 'It's nearest. An' my mother's out, too, an' the hose pipe's right at the bottom of the garden. I bet no one sees us . . .'

It was, however, Ginger's mother, who, returning about a quarter of an hour later, came upon the disgraceful scene – a wild medley of naked boys on the lawn, wrestling and leaping about in the full play of the garden hose, manipulated by Ginger. Their clothes, which they had flung carelessly on the grass beside them, were soaked through . . .

That, of course, and its painful sequel, should have been the end of the A.R.P. as far as William was concerned. He fully intended that it should be. He meant to have no more dealings with it of any kind. He even abandoned a secretly cherished project of turning the spare bedroom into a gas-proof chamber, as a pleasant surprise for his family ('Jolly well serve 'em right now not to have one,' he said bitterly to himself). He glared ferociously at a heading in his father's newspaper, 'A.R.P. Muddle', thinking at first that it must be making fun of his short-lived, but eventful, leadership of the A.R.P. Junior Branch. ('Muddle!' he muttered. 'We didn't do a *thing* that wasn't in the book.

They can go on doin' it for weeks an' weeks an' no one stops 'em, but the minute we *start* they set on us. Well, they'll jolly well be sorry when the war comes, that's all, an' it'll be their own faults.')

If it hadn't been for the local 'black-out', William would not have given the thing another thought except as a faint memory of a glorious day followed by much ill-merited suffering. But the local 'black-out' thrilled and impressed him, and made him long again to take his part in the great national movement. The dark roads, the shuttered windows, the blazing search-lights, the sound of the aeroplanes roaring overhead, stirred his blood, and he wanted to be up and doing – shooting down aeroplanes, or fighting with them in the search-lit sky. He took his air-gun and pointed it upwards between the drawn curtains.

'Bang, bang! That's got 'em,' he muttered with satisfaction. 'That's got 'em all right! Listen to 'em comin' down. That's got another. *An'* another.'

As he dressed the next morning he decided that the failure of his previous attempts at A.R.P. work lay in the large number of its participants.

'When there's a lot of 'em they always start gettin' rough,' he said sternly, scowling at his reflection in the mirror and brushing his hair with almost vindictive energy.

'Always start gettin' rough when there's a lot of 'em. I bet if I'd done somethin' alone it'd've been all right . . . *I bet* it would . . .'

After breakfast he happened to see the *National Service Handbook* lying on his mother's writing desk. It had only arrived a few days before, and he had not had an opportunity of examining it yet. He took it up and turned over the pages with interest. Police . . . Fire Service . . . First Aid . . . Not much he could do . . . Then he began to read with interest the section headed: 'Evacuation of Children from Dangerous Areas'. 'Removing children from the dangers of air attack on crowded cities to districts of greater safety.' Well, he could help with that, all right. Anyone could help with that. An' he'd do it himself, too, not get in a lot of other people. It was that that had messed things up before . . . Hadley would come under the heading of a crowded city, surely . . . It had shops and streets and rows of houses, and it was jolly crowded, especially on market day. And – William threw a glance out of the window – this must be a district of greater safety, all fields and hedges and that sort of thing. Well – he could easily fetch children in here from Hadley. He wouldn't mind doing that. In fact, his spirits rose as he saw himself bringing in a swarm of Hadley children, rather in the manner of the Pied Piper of Hamelin, and establishing them in his home, and those of his friends.

He couldn't do it till there was a war, of course, but he'd do it then, all right. He'd start off as soon as the war broke out. People'd be jolly grateful to him . . .

That afternoon, having nothing much else to do, he set out for Hadley in order to study it in its new light of danger zone. Yes, there were quite a lot of people in the High Street and in the Market Square. It certainly came under the heading of 'crowded city'. He'd collect as many of the children as he could as soon as the war broke out, and escort them at once to the safer sur- roundings of his home. No one could object to his doing something that he was told to do in a book sent out by the Government . . .

Dismissing the subject for a time, he gave his whole attention to examining the windows of Hadley's leading toyshop. He spent several minutes in comparing the dif- ferent merits of a *6d.* pistol and a *6d.* trumpet – a purely academic process, as he possessed no money at all. Having, after deep thought, decided in favour of the pistol, he was just about to move on to the sweetshop next door in order to make a theoretical choice between the wares in that window, too, when he banged into two chil- dren who were standing watching him. They were stolid, four-square children and exactly alike – with red hair and placid, amiable expressions.

'Well, what're you starin' at?' demanded William truc-ulently.

'You,' they said simultaneously.

'Anythin' funny about me?' he said threateningly.

'Yes,' they said.

This took the wind out of his sails, and he said rather flatly:

'Well, you're jolly funny yourselves, come to that. What've you done to your hair?'

'What've you done to yours?'

'Funny colour for hair, yours.'

'Well, yours is all stickin' up.'

'You look like a couple of Guy Fawkes.'

'So do you. You look like two couples.'

Friendly relations having been thus established, William continued:

'How old are you?'

'Seven.'

'Both of you?'

'Yes, we're twins. How old are you?'

'Eleven. What's your names?'

'Hector an' Herbert. What's yours?'

'William. Where d'you live?'

'There. In that street.'

William's gaze followed the direction of the pointing

'WELL, WHAT'RE YOU STARIN' AT?' DEMANDED WILLIAM
TRUCULENTLY.
'YOU,' THEY SAID SIMULTANEOUSLY.

fingers. It was one of the narrow, crowded streets that ran
off from the High Street – one of the streets, without
doubt, from which William would have to rescue his child

protégés when the time of emergency should come. It occurred to him that he might as well explain matters to the twins. There wouldn't be much time for explanation when war had actually broken out. He assumed his sternest expression and most authoritative manner.

'You've gotter be 'vacuated when war comes,' he said.

'We've been it,' said Herbert. 'Our arms swelled up somethink awful.'

'I don't mean that sort of 'vacuation,' said William. 'I mean, took out. Took out of crowded cities to districts of greater safety, same as it says in the book. 'Cause of bombs an' things.'

Light dawned upon the twins. Their eyes gleamed. They leapt excitedly up and down on the pavement with squeals of joy. They had had staying with them recently some cousins from London who had been evacuated in the last crisis and who had told them thrilling tales of camp life – games, entertainment, unlimited food of unusual kinds, and a glorious crumbling of the whole fabric of discipline.

'Coo! Lovely!' said Hector.

Herbert looked expectantly at William and said simply:

'Come on. Let's start now.'

William was somewhat taken aback by their matter-of-fact acceptance of the position. He had expected to have to explain, persuade, cajole . . .

'Well . . .' he began uncertainly, but Herbert had already taken his hand.

'Come on,' he said urgently. 'Let's start off. Shall we have sausage an' fried potato for breakfast, same as they had?'

'Well . . .' began William again, and then thought suddenly that he might as well take them up to the village. It would show them the way. They would be able to help him bring the other children when the war broke out. It would save time then to have two, at any rate, who knew just where to go.

'All right,' he ended. 'We might as well jus' go there . . .'

They accompanied him joyously up the hill to the village, telling him excitedly all the stories that their cousins had told them.

'They had a tug-of-war.'

'They had sports every afternoon.'

'They had picnics.'

'They had treacle tart.'

'They jus' had a few lessons, but not real 'uns.'

'It was jus' like Christmas.'

'They made as much noise as they liked, an' no one stopped them.'

They chattered so much that William could hardly get a word in till they reached the gate of his house.

There he stopped and said a little lamely:

'Well, this is it. You'll know where to come now, won't you?'

'But we've come,' said Hector simply. 'We're here, aren't we?' He opened the gate. 'Come on.'

William hesitated, then suddenly remembered that his mother was out, that it was Cook's afternoon off and that the housemaid had been summoned to attend a sick aunt. 'You'll be out all afternoon, won't you, William?' his mother had said. 'I'll be home in time to get the tea, but it's no good your coming back before then, because there'll be no one in.'

The Browns' house contained a cellar, which was used for the purpose of storing such things as coal, potatoes and Mrs Brown's pickled eggs. William had heard his family discussing the possibility of using this as an air-raid shelter, and had already decided to house his evacuated children in it during air raids. It wouldn't do any harm to show it to the twins. It seemed silly to bring them all this way and then not show them their air-raid shelter . . .

Though the front door was shut, a spare key was always kept under the edge of the mat in the porch for the use of such members of the family as happened to have forgotten their own. It wouldn't take a minute just to unlock the door and show the twins their air-raid shelter. It couldn't possibly do any harm. No one could object to that. In any case, no one need know . . .

'I'll jus' show you the place,' he said.

He took the key from under the mat, unlocked the door, and led the twins into the hall.

'What time's tea?' said Herbert, wiping his feet on the mat.

'We're going to have some games first, aren't we?' said Hector anxiously.

'Well . . .' said William, beginning to feel somewhat overwhelmed by his responsibilities. 'I bet I can find you somethin' to eat, an' p'raps we can have a game of some sort . . . Anyway, I've gotter show you the way to the cellar first. It's down here.'

He opened a door under the stairs, revealing a flight of stone steps.

'Coo!' said Herbert, with obvious approval. 'That's jolly fine!'

He was a boy of an adventurous turn of mind, and found this, to him, novel subterranean world preferable even to the open-air camp-life described by his cousins.

'I bet I find some hidden treasure,' he added.

'Bags me find some, too,' said Hector.

They went down the steps to the cellar. The light which came from a small window, lit by a grating above, was dim and ghostlike. There was a heap of coal in one corner, a sack of potatoes in another, and a sack of carrots in another. (Mr Brown had lately read an article on the nutritive value of carrots and had bought a sack from a friend at Covent Garden.) In another stood two pails containing Mrs Brown's pickled eggs. A broken step-ladder, a bottomless bucket, and a broken clothes-basket completed the furniture.

'You see, you'll be here while there's an air-raid goin' on,' explained William.

The twins continued to survey their surroundings with approval.

'It looks a jolly int'restin' place,' said Herbert. 'Where do we sleep?'

'Well – upstairs, I suppose,' said William, who hadn't considered that question yet.

'We'd better go back for our night things now, hadn't we?' said Hector. 'We didn't bring anythin' with us.'

It dawned on William for the first time that the twins considered themselves permanently evacuated, that they were contemplating forming part of the Brown ménage for an indefinite period. Just as he opened his mouth to correct this misapprehension, the front-door bell sounded through the house. He froze and waited in silence. It sounded again. Quickly he considered the situation. If he didn't answer it, it would probably continue to ring for some time. Moreover, the visitor, whoever it was, might, if left there too long, notice through the grating mysterious signs of life in the cellar below. Better perhaps go and answer the door, and say that his mother was not at home. Then the visitor would go away and he would be left in peace to deal with his evacuated twins.

'Wait a minute,' he whispered, and went quickly up the short flight of stairs to the hall. There he carefully closed the door leading to the cellar and opened the front door. His expression was stern and forbidding.

'My mother—' he began with a fierce scowl, and stopped.

Miss Milton stood on the doorstep, holding a small paper bag in her hand.

'Oh, good afternoon, William,' she said.

''Afternoon,' responded William, scowling yet more ferociously. 'My mother's out. Everyone's out but me.'

'Oh, that's all right, dear,' said Miss Milton. 'I've just brought something for her Pound Day. She asked us to send them round in the morning, I know, but I've not had a second till now.'

William remembered vaguely that streams of groceries had been arriving all morning for the Pound Day of a Girls' Hostel in Hadley, for which Mrs Brown collected local subscriptions. William hadn't been interested then, and he wasn't interested now. He held out his hand for the parcel.

'A' right,' he said shortly. 'I'll give it her.'

'I'd like to write her a note about it, if I may,' said Miss Milton, stepping past William's solidly obstructive form into the hall, and making her way to the drawing-room. William followed, his expression one vast silent protest.

She sat down at the writing table, took a piece of Mrs Brown's writing paper, and began the note.

'You see, dear,' she explained to William, as she wrote, 'I've brought rice because I thought that probably no one else would think of it, but I wanted to tell her that if she'd rather have the unpolished kind – they say it's more nourishing, unpolished, you know, though I could never fancy it myself, it looks so dirty – but if she'd rather have the unpolished kind the grocer will change it . . .'

'I'll tell her that,' said William gruffly. 'You needn't write it all down.'

His ears were strained anxiously for suspicious sounds from below. Miss Milton was a notorious busybody. She never left anything alone till she'd got to the bottom of it.

'That's very kind of you, dear,' said Miss Milton

serenely, as she continued her note, 'but you know, verbal messages are so apt to get distorted. I think it's so much better to have things in black and white.' She murmured her words aloud as she wrote. 'They'll – change – it – for – unpolished – if – you—' Then she stopped suddenly and sat listening, her whole body tense. The worst had happened. Hector and Herbert were exploring the cellar just underneath her with shouts of rapture. Their actual words could not be heard, but William could tell that they were acclaiming their discoveries to each other in careless glee.

Miss Milton put down her pen and looked at William.

'I thought, dear,' she said in a low voice, still listening intently to the mysterious sounds, 'that you were alone in the house.'

'Yes, I am,' said William.

'Then what's that?' said Miss Milton.

'What?' said William, deciding to brazen it out.

'Those voices.'

'What voices?' said William, exchanging his forbidding scowl for an expression of exaggerated bewilderment.

'Can't you – hear?' said Miss Milton, dropping her voice still further.

'Hear what?' said William, whose expression now suggested that of an amiable half-wit.

'Voices,' said Miss Milton again, looking about the

29

room. 'They seem to come from all around me.'

William realised with something of relief that Miss Milton's sense of hearing was not very clear, and that she was not aware that the Brown house contained a cellar.

'It's prob'ly an echo,' he said hopefully.

'Echo?' said Miss Milton, a little tartly. 'My dear boy, an echo of *what*?'

'Well, anythin',' said William. 'Echoes come from anywhere, you know. It might be jus' people talkin' miles off, an' it – well, it's just sort of echoes.'

'That's nonsense, my dear boy,' said Miss Milton, so firmly that William decided to abandon the echo theory.

'It's prob'ly rats, then,' he tried next. 'Rats or the wind. I've often noticed rats an' wind sound jus' like people talkin'.'

'But *you* hear nothing,' said Miss Milton. 'You just said that you heard nothing.'

'No, I can't hear anythin',' said William. ''Cept – well, 'cept jus' a bit of rats an' wind.'

Miss Milton listened again, still more intently, while the voices of Hector and Herbert rose muffled but vociferous from below. William cleared his throat, then coughed loud and long, but not quite loud or long enough to drown the twins' exultant yells. Then he looked at Miss Milton in surprise. Her air of bewilderment had changed to one of happy ecstasy that sat oddly upon her plain, matter-of-fact, pince-nezed face.

'Tell me, dear,' she said. 'Do other people hear these sounds?'

'Well, yes,' said William, anxious to take her mind off the subject as quickly as possible. 'Some people do. Some people hear them all right. It's jus' somethin' wrong with their ears,' he went on in sudden inspiration. 'That's what it is. People with somethin' wrong with their ears hear 'em. It's nothin' axshully serious, of course,' he added hastily. 'They jus' hear voices like that when there's some-thin' wrong with their ears, that's all.'

But the expression of ecstasy did not fade from Miss Milton's face.

'Oh, no, it's not that, dear boy,' she said, in a dreamy, far-away voice. 'It's not that. My mother was the seventh child of a seventh child, and, though this is the first man-ifestation I've actually experienced, I've always known that it must be there somewhere.' She looked about her with a blandly complacent smile, as the voices of Hector and Herbert arose again – now in sudden altercation. 'Voices everywhere . . . All around me . . .' She patted William's head. 'Be thankful that you do not hear them, dear boy. A gift like that is a great responsibility . . . Well,' she drew herself up and spoke in a quick, brisk voice, 'one still has to live in the material world of everyday life, has one not? One must not forget that. One must not allow any manifestation of another world to cause one to forget one's duty in this one, and my next duty is to go to see Mrs Bott about mending the surplices. She always seems to be away from home her week, and I've decided to nail her down. Be sure your mother gets my note, won't you? Well . . .' She drifted into the hall and paused as a loud shout from Hector floated up from the cellar. 'They seem to follow me,' she said, with a seraphic smile, 'to move with me as I move . . . Well,' resuming her brisk voice, 'as I said, one must not neglect one's duty . . .'

To William's relief she had now reached the front door. He watched her drift down the drive, turn round anxiously when she reached the gate, then reassured by a yell from the twins, pass happily on her way.

'Corks!' gasped William, when she was safely out of sight. 'Corks! I thought she was never goin'. I'll get 'em out quick 'fore anyone else comes.'

He hastened down the cellar steps to find a hilarious potato fight going on. A large King Edward hurled by Hector at Herbert hit him on the nose as he reached the bottom of the stairs. He firmly resisted the temptation to join in the fight.

'We're havin' a jolly good time,' panted Herbert. 'It's a

jolly fine place. I wish we'd got a place like this in our house. We're pretendin' we're smugglers an' pirates in a cave. We're having a jolly good fight.'

'Listen,' said William urgently. 'You've gotter go home now. This was only a sort of practice. You—'

At that moment the front-door bell rang again.

'Corks!' groaned William. 'S'like a bad dream.'

Once more he weighed the advantages of answering and not answering the bell, and once more decided in favour of answering. But he must secure the twins' silence. Another visitor might not be ready to ascribe their raucous young voices to psychic origins.

'Look here,' he said hoarsely. 'I've gotter go for a minute. You've not gotter make a noise. Will you promise to be quiet while I'm away?'

'Is it the enemy?' said Hector, with eager interest. 'We've been sayin' p'raps the enemy'd come. When will they start droppin' bombs?'

Herbert threw a potato at the small, grimy window, breaking one of the panes, and shrieked excitedly.

'The enemy! The enemy! The enemy! Bomb! Bomb!'

'Shut up,' said William fiercely. 'It *is* the enemy, an' they *will* drop bombs if you start makin' a noise. If you're quiet they'll go away. P'raps they're goin' away now.' He listened hopefully, but the only sound that broke the silence was another and more imperious peal of the front-door bell. He sighed. 'No, they're not goin' away. Well, it'll be all right s'long as you're quiet, but if you start kickin' up a row they'll start droppin' bombs.'

'What'll we do if they come down here?' said Hector.

'Pelt 'em with potatoes,' shouted Herbert gleefully.

'Shut *up*!' said William.

Another peal of the front-door bell told him that the visitor was of the sort that never owns defeat, so, with another stern admonition to the twins not to speak till he returned, he hastened again up the cellar steps to the front door. Mrs Monks, the vicar's wife, stood there with a small grocer's paper bag in her hand. The scowl with which William greeted her was more repellent than ever.

''Fraid my mother's out,' he muttered gruffly.

Mrs Monks pushed him on to one side and sailed placidly into the hall.

'I want to leave this for the Pound Day,' she said, 'and write her an apology for not having left it this morning, as she asked us to.'

'You needn't stay'n write her a note,' said William with a note almost of pleading in his voice. At present there was silence below, but at any moment, he felt, pandemonium might break out again. 'I'll tell her. I'll 'splain. You can go right away now. I'll 'splain all right.'

'My dear William,' said Mrs Monks, 'I never believe in leaving explanations to a third party. In any case, I owe her an apology, and I must make it as nearly in person as possible. I certainly can't send it verbally, even by you. Indeed, I know how often children of your age either forget to give messages, or give them in a completely garbled form.'

She laid down her paper bag and handbag on the hall chest side by side, and sailed into the drawing-room taking her place at Mrs Brown's writing table.

'I didn't *forget* to bring my pound of rice this morning,' she went on, 'but my housemaid was taken ill, and I haven't had a moment till now. Not a *moment*. I got rice, by the way, because I thought that probably no one else would think of it.' Her pen moved rapidly over the paper as she spoke. William stood by her, tense and rigid, listening with every nerve for sounds from below. But all was still and silent. Evidently Hector and Herbert had taken his words to heart. Once he thought he heard someone moving in the hall, but the sound ceased almost at once, and it was plain that Mrs Monks heard nothing.

'There!' she said, signing her name with a flourish. 'See she gets that, won't you? Well, I must hurry off now.' She collected her handbag from the hall chest and sailed to the front door. 'Be *sure* you give her my note . . . *Good*bye.'

William heaved a sigh of relief as she sailed down the

drive and disappeared into the road. The danger was over. He could now dispose of the twins before his mother came back, and— His heart sank again. Another figure was coming up the drive, carrying a grocer's paper bag. Too late even to pretend that there was no one in the house, as he had decided to in case of future interruptions, for she had seen him and was waving to him gaily. It was Miss Thompson, who lived with her aunt at The Larches. She was small and fluttery, like a bird, and she wore a hat with a perky little feather sticking up in front like a bird's top-knot.

'Is your mother in?' she said breathlessly, as she reached the front door. 'Aren't I *naughty*? I quite forgot about bringing my pound this morning. I've no excuse at all. I just forgot! I bought a new hat in Hadley this morning, and I'm afraid it drove everything else out of my mind.' She fluttered into the hall and looked at herself in the mirror. 'It's rather nice, isn't it?' she said. 'I thought it was a bit too young at first, but the woman persisted that it wasn't. She said everyone was wearing them, and that it was *quite* suitable. It's just a *leetle* on the small side. It gave me a headache even in the shop, and it's coming on again now. I must take it back to be stretched. I'll just slip it off now while I write my note of apology to your mother. It will give my head a rest.'

'I'll tell her,' said William desperately. 'You needn't write. You can go home an' rest your head prop'ly . . .'

But she wasn't listening to him. She was putting her hat and grocer's bag on the hall chest, side by side, and chattering away in her birdlike inconsequential fashion.

'I see I'm not the only naughty one. I do hope your mother will forgive me. Such a little scatter-brain, I always am! I got rice. I thought that probably no one else would think of it. And it's so wholesome. Whole tribes live on it in India. Now may I just go into the drawing-room, and write my little note? I *do* hope she won't be cross with me. I thought of it first thing this morning and then, as I said, the hat drove it clean out of my mind. May I sit here and use a piece of her notepaper? "Dear – Mrs – Brown . . ."'

William watched her helplessly, his body rigid, his ears strained. Once he thought again that he heard stealthy sounds outside the room, but decided it must be his imagination.

'"Please – forgive—"' said Miss Thompson, slowly ending her note, '"your – scatter-brained – friend – Louisa – Thompson." There!' She fastened up the envelope. 'Now I must fly. *Literally* fly. My aunt wanted to have tea early today and—' She glanced at the clock. 'My *goodness*! I'm late already. I shouldn't have come till after tea. What a *scatter-brain* I am! Forgive me, dear. I can't stop to hear all your news, though I'd love to.' She fluttered into the hall, snatched up her hat without looking at it, perched it on her head, said, 'Goodbye, goodbye, good-bye! Give my love to your dear mother,' and fluttered off down the drive.

William closed the door and drew a long, deep breath.

'Crumbs!' he said, in a tone of heartfelt relief.

The next step was plain. Now that the coast was clear all he had to do was to bring the twins from their hiding-place and speed them on their homeward way. But, before he'd had time even to reach the cellar door, there was the sound of a key in the lock, and his mother entered.

'Hello, dear!' she said. 'I never thought you'd get back before me. I came back earlier than I intended, anyway . . . Oh, dear! Rice again. No one seems to be able to think of anything else but rice. Still, the grocer says he'll change it . . . Now there's only you and me, dear, so we'll have a nice cosy tea together. And you'll help me get it ready, won't you? You can be such a help when you like.'

Despairingly, he watched Mrs Brown hang her hat and coat on the hatstand, then read the three notes that were on the hall chest with the three bags of rice. He could hear faint sounds from the cellar below. They began to increase in volume.

'Mother,' he said, speaking in a loud, booming voice, in order to drown them, 'wouldn't you like to go an' lie down for a bit while I get tea? Jus' about five minutes.' (He could easily get rid of the twins in five minutes.) 'You – you look a bit tired to me. You look 's if it'd do you good to have a bit of a lie-down while I get tea.'

Mrs Brown gazed at him tenderly, deeply touched by this proof of his affection and considerateness, storing up the incident in her mind in order to tell her husband when he came home from work. ('I'm always telling you that you don't do William justice, dear. Now just listen to what he said to me when I came in this afternoon . . .')

'That's a very kind thought, dear,' she said, 'but I'm not feeling at all tired, and I certainly won't let you get the tea all alone. Many hands make light work, you know. Now I'll put the kettle on, and you get out the tablecloth and—'

'Mother,' said William with the urgency of desperation (again his ears, strained to attention, had caught those faint sounds from below), 'it seemed to me some-one'd stole a lot of tools from our tool shed this afternoon. Seemed to me quite a lot of them'd gone when I came in.' (If only he could get her out of the house as long as it would take to go to the tool shed and back, it would give him time to drag the twins up from their retreat and hustle them off home.)

'What had gone, dear?' Mrs Brown said placidly.

'Well,' temporised William, 'I can't say *quite* what'd

gone. I didn't count 'xactly. I only saw that *some'd* gone. I thought I'd better tell you . . .'

'I expect you're mistaken, dear,' said Mrs Brown, bustling about the kitchen, quite unmoved by the news. 'You're always imagining things. I'll look after tea but I'm certainly going to have a cup of tea before I do anything else. Anyway, if they're gone, they're gone, and a few minutes won't matter here or there . . . Have you got the cloth out, dear?'

'Mother . . .' said William. (He was going to tell her that he thought he'd heard the boiler burst just before she came in. That should get her up to the loft at any rate.) But at that moment there came another ring at the front-door bell.

'See who it is, dear,' called his mother.

William went to the door. Miss Milton entered. There was a tense, keyed-up look on her face.

'I'm so sorry,' she said in a tense, keyed-up voice to Mrs Brown, who had come out of the kitchen to see who it was. 'I'm terribly sorry, but I *must* make sure.'

'Make sure?' said Mrs Brown.

'Yes,' said Miss Milton. 'It was here I heard them. They seemed to follow me to the gate, then stopped. I've not heard them since. I *had* to come back here and – make sure. Can I still hear them here? I know I did before. Often that – extra sense, shall we call it? – functions erratically, but one must do what one can to understand it, to regularise it . . . I felt that I *must* make sure whether I could still hear them here . . .'

'Them?' faltered Mrs Brown.

She'd always known that Miss Milton was a little eccentric, but – well, really, eccentric was almost too mild a word for this.

'The voices,' said Miss Milton.

'The voices?'

'Yes.'

Miss Milton had stridden into the drawing-room, and was standing there in the middle of the room, every muscle taut as if poised for flight.

'I heard them here,' she said dreamily, 'only a few minutes ago. Voices. All round me.'

She listened, but there was no sound. The twins had evidently discovered some silent occupation for the moment. Mrs Brown was too much bewildered for speech, and William realised the uselessness of it.

'Strange!' said Miss Milton. 'Either the gift has deserted me or—'

At that moment came another interruption. It was Mrs Monks. Admitted by William, she sailed into the drawing-room, her face set and stern, and, opening the small handbag she carried, drew out three or four carrots.

'What's the meaning of this?' she said severely.

Mrs Brown sat down upon the nearest chair.

'What on earth is happening?' she said helplessly.

'I came here a few minutes ago,' said Mrs Monks, 'to leave my rice and write a note of apology—'

'Fancy you thinking of rice!' put in Miss Milton, who had now decided that the gift had deserted her.

'I laid my handbag on the hall chest while I came in to write my note,' continued Mrs Monks, ignoring Miss Milton. 'I had met the organist just before I reached your gate and had opened my bag to consult my diary because we were discussing the most suitable day for the choir treat. The bag then held its usual contents – my purse, stamp book, engagement diary and – er – a small powder compact. As I said, I laid it down on your hall chest for a matter of – say – five minutes and when I got home I found that it contained – *these*!' She held out the carrots dramatically.

Mrs Brown looked at William. William looked at the carrots and understood now only too well those faint sounds he had heard in the hall while Mrs Monks was writing her note . . .

'William!' said Mrs Brown reproachfully.

With obvious reluctance, Mrs Monks exonerated William.

'Well, it couldn't have been William,' she said. 'Not *actually* William, at least. William was in here with me all the time.'

'But who could have done it, then?' said Mrs Brown. 'William, you didn't bring any of your friends home with you, did you?'

'No, Mother,' said William, assuring himself that neither Hector nor Herbert came under that category. 'No, Mother, I didn't bring any of my friends home.'

'But I can't *think*—' began Mrs Brown, when Miss Thompson entered. She entered in her usual birdlike, fluttering manner, but she suggested now a bird in deep distress. She wore perched on her head a little plain, untrimmed hat.

'I found the front door open, and so I just came in,' she said. 'Mrs Brown, I don't know *what* to do. I can't think *what's* happened . . .'

'Happened?' said Mrs Brown, in a faint voice.

'To my hat,' said Miss Thompson. 'I only bought it this morning. I *came* in it when I came to bring my rice.' ('Rice!' put in Mrs Monk, and Miss Milton in indignant surprise.) 'It had a band of ribbon round it and a little feather in the front. William knows it had. He saw it. I showed it him. I looked at it in the glass. I took it off because it was making my head ache, and put it on the chest while I came in here to write my note, and then I put it on again – Oh, very carelessly and without looking because I'm such a scatter-brain, you know – but when I got home and took it off I found that the trimming had gone.'

The room spun round Mrs Brown. She caught hold of the table next to her to keep it still.

William's face wore a fixed and glassy look of horror. Gosh! They'd been up both times. They'd taken the things out of Mrs Monks's handbag and the trimming from Miss Thompson's hat.

'The trimming gone?' repeated Mrs Brown feebly.

'Yes,' said Miss Thompson. 'The trimming gone. It was quite untrimmed when I got home. It couldn't have *fallen* off. A band of ribbon and a feather can't *fall* off a hat while it's on the head. I know I'm a scatter-brain, but I'm quite sure of that. It must have been taken off, and it must have been taken off here while I was writing my note . . . And it couldn't have been William, because he was with me all the time.'

Mrs Brown raised a hand to her head. She looked from the carrots that Mrs Monks was still holding out accusingly, to the plain, straw hat in Miss Thompson's small, clawlike hand.

'I – I don't understand,' she said. 'I mean – who *could* it have been?'

THE ROOM SPUN ROUND MRS BROWN. SHE CAUGHT HOLD
OF THE TABLE NEXT TO HER TO KEEP IT STILL.

'A poltergeist,' said Miss Milton, in a tone of deep satisfaction. 'I've read about them in psychic papers. That was what I heard, and that was what put carrots in Mrs Monks's bag and took the trimming off Miss Thompson's hat.'

WILLIAM'S FACE WORE A FIXED AND GLASSY LOOK OF
HORROR.

'Stuff and nonsense!' said Mrs Monks rudely. 'Anyway,
what I want to know is, where my purse and engagement
diary have got to, and where Miss Thompson's feather is?
That's the question.'

Mrs Brown made a supreme effort to recover her fac-
ulties.

'William,' she said, 'do you know anything at all about this?'

William was saved from answering by a loud noise from below. It sounded like – and probably was – someone sliding down a heap of coal.

They stared at each other in silence for a few seconds, then Mrs Brown went from the room to the cellar door and stood there listening. The others followed slowly.

'There's someone in the cellar,' she said at last, her face paling as she turned to them. 'I can hear them moving about quite plainly.'

A thief in the cellar was something definite, something one could, to a certain extent at any rate, deal with, and Mrs Brown's usual matter-of-fact manner returned to her. With a quick movement she twisted the key in the lock, then turned to William.

'William, go round to the police station at once and fetch Sergeant Perkins. It's no use ringing them up,' she went on to the others, 'because, if you do, the stupid one always answers and he's deaf as well. Run as fast as you can, William. Tell Sergeant Perkins that I've got a man – say a *dangerous* man – locked in the cellar, and that he'd better bring help in case he's violent. I was saying only the other day that that cellar's not safe. A thief could so easily remove the grating and force the window and then conceal himself there till everyone was in bed. Hurry up, William! Don't stand dawdling there. Run all the way . . .'

William went out of the front door, his face set like the face of a sleepwalker. Long ago he had given up all hope of being able to control the situation. He was now the blind tool of Fate . . .

The three women stood by the cellar door, watching the keyhole anxiously, as though it might unlock itself if not kept under close observation.

'You did *lock* it, didn't you?' said Miss Milton apprehensively. 'It would be rather a catastrophe if it *had* been locked and you'd unlocked it.'

'No,' said Mrs Brown. 'It's all right.' She tried the key again. 'It's quite safe.'

'I wonder if he knows we know,' said Mrs Monks. 'I hope he isn't *planning* anything.' Then a sudden thought struck her and she said: 'But, Mrs Brown, that doesn't explain the carrots.'

'Nor my feather,' said Miss Thompson.

Then suddenly there came from the cellar another sound of falling coal, followed by a peal of unmistakably childish laughter.

'It's – children,' gasped Mrs Brown.

'So it is,' said Mrs Monks. Her nervousness vanished abruptly. Children. She knew how to deal with children.

She could control a whole Sunday school by the flicker of an eyelash. There was no choirboy in existence so unquellable that she could not quell him at once . . . She seemed to grow several inches taller as she assumed her official manner.

'Let me deal with this,' she said. 'To begin with, at any rate. I'll go down first, alone. If I need help I'll call . . .'

'But, Mrs Monks—' began Mrs Brown anxiously.

Mrs Monks paid no attention to her. With the air of a general at the head of a large army she marched down the cellar steps. At the bottom the dim light from the grating showed her the whole scene in a moment – Herbert as a Red Indian, wearing round his head the trimming of Miss Thompson's hat, Hector as the Pale Face (his face paled by Mrs Monks's powder compact), and, ranged in a small box, the contents of Mrs Monks's handbag, by means of which the Pale Face had been purchasing native food (such as carrots and potatoes). Many half-eaten carrots lay about them on the floor. Their persons revealed generous traces of the coal-heap, which they had utilised for 'shooting the rapids'. But this scene lasted only a moment. William had warned the twins that the enemy might come, and the twins had prepared a heap of ammunition in readiness for the contingency. No sooner had Mrs Monks taken in this amazing scene than one of Mrs Brown's pickled eggs caught her full on the forehead, and another on her mouth, which she was opening for a majestic reproof. Almost immediately afterwards a large piece of coal struck her on the chest. Mrs Monks was a brave woman. She had once shoo'ed out a dangerous bull that had strayed into the Vicarage garden, and it had obeyed her meekly. But she was winded, choked and blinded. Dripping with coal and egg, she staggered up the cellar steps to rejoin the other three. They stared at her in blank dismay.

'There are two children down there,' she said indistinctly, but with as much dignity as could possibly be mustered in the circumstances. 'Two children. Quite small, but – I think I'll sit down for a moment. I seem to have swallowed an egg shell . . .'

From below came the voices of the twins, now unrestrained and exultant.

'We're bombing the enemy,' they shouted. 'We're bombing the enemy! The enemy! The enemy! We're bombing the enemy!'

'Come along, Miss Thompson,' said Mrs Brown firmly. 'We must do something at once.'

They descended the steps – only to return a few moments later in much the same condition as Mrs Monks.

'There's no getting near them,' gasped Mrs Brown, wiping egg out of her eye.

'The little villains!' panted Miss Thompson. 'My poor feather! Oh, dear, I've swallowed such a big piece of coal. I hope it won't do me any harm.'

'Of course it won't,' said Mrs Monks curtly. 'Carbon's good for the digestion.'

From below the exultant shouts increased in volume to the accompaniment of breaking eggs. Herbert and Hector were evidently carrying on a glorious fight.

'Bombing the enemy!' and they continued to shout: 'Bomb! Bomb! Bomb! Bomb! Bomb!'

'My poor eggs!' moaned Mrs Brown. 'I put down eight dozen.'

Then William returned. He had no suspicion of recent developments, and had had the sudden and brilliant idea of pretending that Hector and Herbert had fallen through the grating accidentally and become imprisoned in the cellar through no fault of their own or his.

But the sight of the three figures in the hall took away his power of speech and, before he had recovered it, Mrs Brown spoke in a firm voice.

'William, I'll ask you about this later. But for the present go down into the cellar at once and bring up those two children.'

William obeyed. There was nothing else to do. He went down to the cellar and stopped the egg-battle.

'We've bombed the enemy,' sang Hector, and:

'Is the war over now?' asked Herbert.

William assured them grimly that as far as they were concerned the war was over, and escorted them up the cellar stairs. Plastered with coal and egg they were still dimly recognisable as human beings. Miss Thompson pounced upon Herbert and took her hat trimming from his head.

'It'll need cleaning, of course,' she said, examining it, 'but I don't think it's damaged beyond repair.'

Mrs Monks fixed them with a stern eye.

'*Why* did you put carrots in my bag?' she said.

Then Ethel and Robert entered. They had just come from their A.R.P. class. Ethel had been practising bandaging, and Robert had been listening to a lecture on decontamination.

There was a jagged cut on Hector's temple caused by an unusually resistant egg shell. It was exactly the size and shape of the cut on which Ethel had just been practising. She seized on him with gleaming eyes and began to hustle him upstairs.

'I don't know who you are,' she said, 'but I'm going to bandage that cut. Come on.'

The last egg thrown at Herbert had evidently been a bad one. He stank to Heaven . . . It was just such an object

– blackened by smoke, soaked in noxious gases – on which Robert had imagined himself practising the art of decontamination.

'And I don't know who *you* are, but I'm going to decontaminate you.'

'Yes!' said William bitterly, thinking of his own ill-fated attempt at A.R.P. work. '*They* c'n do it all right. No one stops *them*.'

Mrs Brown watched helplessly as Ethel and Robert swept the twins upstairs before them. The spirits of the twins were still undaunted.

'Aren't we having a lovely time, Hector?' said Herbert.

'Yes,' said Hector happily. 'I like wars.'

Mrs Brown watched till they were out of sight, then turned slowly to the spot from which William had spoken.

But William was no longer there.

William had decided that the time had come to try a spot of evacuation on his own account.

CHAPTER 2

WILLIAM DOES HIS BIT

WILLIAM was finding the war a little dull. Such possibilities as the black-out and other war conditions afforded had been explored to the full and were beginning to pall. He had dug for victory with such mistaken zeal – pulling up as weeds whole rows of young lettuces and cabbages – that he had been forbidden to touch spade, fork or hoe again. He had offered himself at a recruiting office in Hadley, and, though the recruiting sergeant had been jovial and friendly, and had even given him a genuine regimental button, he had refused to enrol him as a member of His Majesty's Forces.

'You're not quite big enough,' he had said. 'There's very strict regulations about size.'

'I grow quick,' pleaded William. 'I'm always growin' out of things.'

'Not quite quick enough for us,' said the sergeant firmly.

'Well, can't I be a drummer boy?' said William. 'I can make a jolly fine noise on a drum. An aunt of mine said it made her head ache for weeks. I bet it'd scare ole Hitler off all right.'

'No vacancies for drummer boys at present,' said the sergeant.

'Well, will you let me know when there are?' said William.

'Certainly,' said the sergeant, but he winked at a corporal standing near as he spoke, and William didn't set much store by the promise.

He next wrote to the Premier to offer his services as a spy, but received no answer. Thinking that it had been intercepted by German agents, he wrote again but still received no answer. He decided that he could at any rate practise being a spy, so went out wearing Robert's hat and coat, but, despite the corked moustache that was supposed to conceal his identity, he was instantly recognised by Robert and his ears boxed so soundly that he reluctantly abandoned his spy career.

'Cares more about an ole coat an' hat than winnin' the war,' he muttered indignantly. 'He oughter be put in prison, carin' more for an ole coat an' hat than winnin' the war.'

He had almost given up hope of being allowed to make any appreciable contribution to his country's cause when he heard his family discussing an individual called 'Quisling' who apparently, and in a most mysterious fashion, existed simultaneously in at least a dozen places.

'I bet there's one of 'em in England,' said Robert darkly. 'Getting things ready or *thinking* he's getting things ready . . . Gosh! I'd like to get my hands on him.'

'But who *is* he?' said William.

'Shut *up*!' said Robert. 'They're jolly well going to put a spoke in his wheel in Turkey. They never expected to find him in Holland or Belgium!'

'Holland or *Belgium*?' said William. 'Thought you said he was in Holland or Turkey. Thought—'

'Shut *up*!' said Robert and went on darkly: 'And he's right here in England, too. We'll have to keep our eyes open.'

William was past further query or comment.

He tackled his mother, however, the first time he found her alone.

'I say,' he said, 'who is this Grisling man?'

'Quisling, dear,' corrected his mother.

William waved the objection aside.

'Sounds the same,' he said. 'Anyway he *can't* be in Turkey *an*' Belgium *an*' Holland *an*' England at the same time. No one could. Robert's cracked, sayin' he can be.'

'Well, dear, he's not really the same man,' said Mrs Brown. 'He's a sort of – *type*.'

'What's that?' demanded William. 'Thought it was a kind of dog.'

'No, dear,' said Mrs Brown patiently. 'This particular man was a Norwegian and helped the Germans to get a footing in his country, and other people in other countries who try to do the same, are all called Quisling.'

'Why?' said William. 'Why can't they call them by their real names?'

'They don't know what their real names are.'

'Why don't they ask them?'

'Really, William,' said Mrs Brown helplessly, 'I can't explain it any more. Go out of doors and play.'

'Well, listen,' pleaded William. 'Tell me jus' one thing. How do they do it? How do they get people to let ole Hitler in?'

Mrs Brown sighed resignedly.

'I'm not quite sure, dear. I think they sort of make people believe that they'd have no chance of resisting him and so it's best to let him in. They try to frighten people. At least, I think that's it.'

'Why doesn't the Gov'ment lock 'em up?'

'They don't know who they are.'

'Thought they knew they were called Grisling.'

'No dear, they don't.'

'I 'spose they *pretend* they're called other things jus' to put the Gov'ment right off the scent.'

'Yes, I suppose they do,' said Mrs Brown, settling

down to darn a pile of table napkins.

'They might pretend to be called anythin'.'

'Yes,' agreed Mrs Brown. 'I suppose they might. This linen really ought to have worn better. If it weren't for the war I shouldn't trouble to mend them at all.'

'There might be one here pretendin' to be called anythin'.'

'I suppose so, dear . . . It's partly the laundry, of course. They simply *maul* things.'

'An' I bet no one knows who he is. If they did they'd have him in prison.'

'What are you talking about, dear?' said Mrs Brown, bringing her mind with an effort from the composition of a projected letter of complaint to the laundry.

'Ole Grissel,' said William.

'Grissel? Oh, I know what you mean. He isn't called that, but I've forgotten just for the moment what he is called.'

'Bet I'd catch him all right if I was the Gov'ment.'

'He's not alone, of course, dear. He has a lot of people working under him. It's a very complicated organisation, I believe . . . Now, William, do leave that table napkin alone. It was just a weak place before you started pushing your fingers through it, and now it's a real hole.'

'Well, I'm sorry,' said William. 'I didn't know it was

goin' to go through like that. I hardly pushed at all . . . Well – look here, are they *tryin'* to catch this ole Grissel?'

'I expect so, dear.'

'I bet they're not,' said William darkly. 'I jolly well bet they're not. Why didn't they catch him in Norfolk, then?'

'It was Norway, dear, not Norfolk.'

'Well, why didn't they? I don't b'lieve they're tryin' at all. An' he's goin' about same as you or me. It might be anyone. It might be someone we know. It might be Robert, 'cept that he's not got enough brains for it.'

'Well, William, you can't do anything, so stop worrying about it.'

'*Can't* I?' said William. '*Can't* I do anythin'? You jus' see if I can do anythin'. I bet I can.'

He walked out of the house and down the village street, scowling darkly.

Couldn't he do anything! He'd caught one German spy at the beginning of the war (more by good luck than good management, as even he had to admit), and didn't see why he shouldn't catch another. This was a different sort of spy, but if the Government wasn't catching ole Grissel – well, there was nothing for it but to have a shot himself. Perhaps he was here – *here* in the village or in Hadley or in Marleigh. He'd got to be going round scaring people somewhere all the time, so he might as well be here as anywhere else. His face took on that expression of ferocity that betokened firm resolution. The more he thought about the matter the more convinced he was that old Grissel was somewhere in the neighbourhood. William, in whom the zest of the chase was up-rising fiercely, decided that there was not the slightest doubt that he was here. And if he was here, he'd got to be caught, and, if he'd got to be caught, then William was going to catch him. He realised that he must go very carefully. He had a master criminal to deal with and one who would stick at nothing. But there was not a moment to be lost. He must start at once.

He started by a tour of the village. Much to his disappointment, an exhaustive search revealed nothing suspicious. He was at first tempted to suspect the vicar or the doctor of being ole Grissel in disguise, but after a few moments' reflection, he came reluctantly to the conclusion that their normal routine would leave them little or no time for criminal activities. The doctor, in particular, he was unwilling to cross off his list of suspects. The last draught the doctor had compounded for him, on his pleading that he felt too ill to go to school, had been so nauseous that William considered he had narrowly escaped death by poison.

He turned his steps from the village towards Hadley. There, though he followed several false scents, and annoyed several householders by staring in at their windows, he was no more successful. He retraced his steps to the village and made his way to Marleigh, where he couldn't even find any false scents. Dejectedly and having by now almost but, being William, not quite, given up hope, he went on towards Upper Marleigh.

The main road seemed to be empty except for two women who were approaching each other from opposite directions. William looked at them without interest. He wasn't interested in women at the best of times, and just now he wasn't interested in anything at all except ole Grissel. But, as he passed them, he heard something that made him stop and listen attentively.

'What's the code word today?' he heard one of them ask.

He couldn't hear the answer, but the question was enough. A code word. Spies . . . Members of ole Grissel's gang . . . They looked just two ordinary women – the sort that went to Mothers' Meetings and Women's Institutes – and all the time they were members of ole Grissel's gang. It had been careless of him not to have realised that they might be. Naturally ole Grissel's gang would disguise themselves as people like that to put the Government off the scent. Well, he'd found them now and he must shadow them till he ran ole Grissel himself to earth. He studied the two conspirators with interest. One was carrying a shopping basket and the other a string bag full of vegetables, but they'd probably got revolvers and things hidden among the cabbages and groceries and wouldn't scruple to use them. He drew nearer and, stooping down, pretended to be doing up his shoe lace.

'Aren't greens a price?' one of them was saying and the other replied:

'Yes, aren't they! And there don't seem to be half the lettuces about this year. Ours were no good at all – I can't think why.'

They'd seen him, of course, thought William, and were talking like that to put him off the scent. Or – more probably – they were talking in code. Perhaps 'Aren't greens a price?' meant 'Let's kill Churchill,' and 'There don't seem to be so many lettuces about this year' meant 'Heil Hitler' – or something like that.

They were separating now – each going on her way. For a moment William stood irresolute, wondering which to follow. One was going towards the village, the other – the one who had asked what the code word was – was turning down a side lane off the main road. He decided to follow the second one . . .

She went down the lane and in at the gate of a large building that William knew to be a school. It was the summer holiday and the building was empty. She went round to the side and in at a small door. It must be the headquarters of ole Grissel's gang. A jolly good idea, choosing an empty school in holiday time down a side lane like this. He decided not to follow her into the building. Peaceful and deserted though it looked, it probably bristled with concealed machine-guns and snipers and booby traps. Instead, he would inspect the building as best he could from the cover of a belt of variegated laurel that surrounded it. He dived into the nearest bush just in time, for two other women had just arrived and were going in by the same door as the first. They, too, looked the Mothers' Meeting/Women's Institute type. Evidently that was the particular disguise adopted by this particular band of conspirators . . .

William made his way round one side of the building, still under cover of the laurels. It was disappointing in that it contained no window. Nothing daunted, however, he started on the second side. And there he was rewarded, for he suddenly came upon a screen of sandbags and, creeping round the screen, found a window, covered with black paint but conveniently open at the top. Cautiously he hoisted himself on to the window-sill and peeped in. He saw a cellar-like room, roughly furnished with a long trestle table and some chairs. The women he had seen entering had removed their hats and were taking their

CAUTIOUSLY WILLIAM HOISTED HIMSELF ON TO THE
WINDOW-SILLAND PEEPED IN.

places at the trestle table. Others were putting on their
hats and preparing to depart. William's eyes roved round
the room. A man, who was evidently in charge of proceedings, sat at a small desk covered with papers. Ole
Grissel . . . ole Grissel himself! He didn't look as William
had imagined ole Grissel would look – he was undersized
and stooping and had a small worried moustache – but he
was obviously in charge and so he must be ole Grissel. On
a table just beneath the window a large map was out-
spread. By craning his neck William could see that it was

A MAN, WHO WAS EVIDENTLY IN CHARGE OF PROCEEDINGS,
SAT AT A SMALL DESK COVERED IN PAPERS.

a map of the district. He could see Marleigh and Upper
Marleigh marked on it quite plainly. There were little
flags jotted about. Gosh! They had everything ready for
ole Hitler! He could even see the road marked where his
own home was. Going to hand over his own home to ole
Hitler, were they, he thought, indignantly – with Jumble
and his pet mice and his collection of caterpillars and his
new cricket bat. The idea of this infuriated him more

than any of the previous German outrages. He set his lips grimly. Well, if Hitler thought he was going to get his pet mice and his new cricket bat, he was jolly well mistaken. He realised that two of the women sitting at the trestle table were telephoning. He listened in amazement.

'Wrecked aeroplane causing obstruction in Marleigh Road . . . Fire raging in Pithurst Lane . . . Houses in Hill Road collapsed . . . Marleigh police station blown up . . .'

His eyes and mouth opened wider and wider. There wasn't a word of truth in it from beginning to end. He'd walked along Marleigh Road less than five minutes ago . . . He'd passed Marleigh police station – and even exchanged *badinage* with a stout constable who was sunning himself in the doorway. The school building was in Pithurst Lane, and Hill Road was at the end of it. And all lay peaceful and intact in the summer sunshine, while this gang of Grissel confederates were broadcasting these outrageous lies. Propaganda. That was what it was, of course. Broadcasting lies right and left! Same as old Gobbles. One of the women was moving little flags about on the map.

'I haven't any more incendiary bomb flags, Mr Balham,' she said to the man at the desk.

(William made a mental note of the name ole Grissel was calling himself.)

The man opened his desk and gave her a little box, and

William, to his intense indignation, saw her put one on the road where his own home was. Huh! Ole Hitler was probably thinkin' he'd get his cricket bat by the end of the summer. *Huh!* The women at the telephones read out their pieces of propaganda (the latest was 'electric light main, coal gas main and water mains all damaged. No repair parties available. Gas escaping. Fires in vicinity beyond control.') from sheets of paper and, when they had finished, they handed them to the man at the desk, who put them on to a file. William could have watched this absorbing performance all morning, but an incautious movement made him lose his foothold. He fell down heavily and by no means soundlessly to the ground. After that he deemed it advisable to retire to his screen of laurel. At first he was afraid that the conspirators might send out an emissary to investigate and exact vengeance, but, to his relief, no one came.

He sat in the shelter of a particularly luxuriant laurel and considered his next step. He had discovered the nest of traitors, of course, but that wasn't enough. He must bring them to justice. And he knew that this wasn't as easy as it sounded. He hadn't read crime fiction for nothing. He realised that criminals whose meeting-place is discovered simply vanish from it, leaving no trace, and meet somewhere else. No, he must run the arch-traitor to earth – find out where he lived and all about him – before he attempted to bring him to justice.

He had waited, as it seemed to him, several hours when at last the small, insignificant-looking figure of Mr Balham appeared, coming round the side of the building towards the main gate. William, from his hiding-place, studied his quarry with interest. The drooping moustache was, of course, a disguise. So were the spectacles. The stoop was probably a disguise, too. If he stretched right up he'd be quite a tall man. Well, nearly quite a tall man . . . But he was disappearing down Pithurst Lane now, and William, turning up the collar of his jacket, drawing his cap down over his eyes in the conventional fashion of the sleuth, prepared to follow him. Had Mr Balham chanced to turn round, he would have been much surprised by the antics of the small boy behind him, who dived into the ditch, scrambled along under cover of the hedge, hid behind trees for no apparent reason, and occasionally stopped to place twigs in a complicated pattern by the roadside. (These last were intended as signs to lead future investigators to the scene of the crime if the criminal suddenly whipped round and kidnapped or murdered him.)

Happily unaware that he was being shadowed in this sensational fashion, Mr Balham turned into Hill Road (which he and his fellow conspirators had so recently reported bombed) and, opening the garden gate of a small neat newly-built villa, disappeared inside a small neat newly-painted front door. William stood in the road and stared at it, slightly nonplussed. He'd found out where the traitor lived, and so the moment seemed ripe for bringing him to justice, but he realised that even now the enemy might elude him. He had, in fact, come out into the garden in his shirt sleeves and was pushing a microscopic mowing machine round the microscopic front lawn. It was, of course, all part of the disguise. He was pretending to be an ordinary man, mowing an ordinary lawn, and (he had just stopped to do it) picking ordinary green flies off ordinary rose trees. If he told the police that this man was Grissel, the arch-traitor, they would just laugh at him. No, he must find some actual proof. His eyes wandered over the neat, respectable-looking little house. It was probably full of proof if only he could find it – letters and telegrams in code and confidential documents. Traitors always had confidential documents which they burnt when they saw the police coming. So that, even if William managed to persuade the police to come, the man would see them coming and at once burn all his letters and telegrams and confidential documents. Somehow or other William must get hold of the confidential documents himself . . .

It would be jolly dangerous, of course. Ole Grissel would stick at nothing if he found him looking for them. In most of the crime stories William had read the hero was caught by the villain, but the police arrived in the nick of time. He must arrange for the police to arrive in the nick of time . . .

Mr Balham, A.R.P. Communications Worker, Supervisor of Marleigh Report Centre, put on his slippers and sank down into his favourite armchair with a sigh of relief. He had had a tiring day. First of all there had been the air-raid exercise down at the report centre, and he always found those rather exhausting. Then he had put in two hours' gardening and he always found that extremely exhausting. He was glad to relax and to lose himself in his detective novel. The hero of the novel was alone in his flat when there came a ring at the door. He went to open it and found a policeman there.

'Sorry to disturb you, sir,' said the policeman, 'but we've just received a message asking us to come round here.'

At that moment Mr Balham's own door-bell rang, and he put the book aside with a little 'Tut, tut' of exasperation. Some interruption always seemed to come at the most exciting point of a story. On his way to the door, he thought idly how strange it would be if he found a policeman there saying: 'Excuse me, sir, but—'

He stopped on his way through the hall to straighten a mat, then opened the front door, assuming the forbidding expression of one who wants to get back to his detective novel as quickly as possible.

A policeman stood there.

'Excuse me, sir,' he said, 'but—'

Mr Balham was so much astounded that he didn't hear the end of the sentence and had to ask the policeman to repeat it.

'We've had a message asking us to come round here.'

The hall whirled round Mr Balham for a moment, but with an effort he caught hold of it and put it right way up.

'I beg your pardon,' he said, wondering if he had dropped off over the book and this were one of those fantastic dreams he had occasionally.

'We had a message to come round here,' repeated the policeman.

'I never sent any such message,' said Mr Balham, looking down at his legs in sudden apprehension and being reassured by the sight of his neat and decent grey flannel trousers. The oddest things happened to him in his dreams sometimes!

'Well, it was certainly a queer sort of message,' the policeman was saying. 'Wouldn't give no name and sounded to me like a disguised voice. Told us to send round here in half an hour's time. Practical joker, probably – you'd be surprised the number we get – but it was on my beat so I said I'd look in.'

'Well, I certainly never sent for you,' said Mr Balham firmly, 'so it must be a practical joke.'

'Probably,' said the policeman, 'but now I'm here I might as well have a look round.'

Entering the house he began a tour of inspection, followed by Mr Balham, who had now come to the conclusion that this was no dream, but a coincidence, such as people wrote to the papers about and recount in clubs. He was wishing that he'd finished the chapter before the police came. It would be interesting to know what the police discovered in the hero's flat.

Well, certainly there was nothing to discover here . . . But he was mistaken. There was something to discover. For at that moment the policeman threw open the dining-room door and discovered a small boy kneeling in front of the open sideboard cupboard, surrounded by silver teapot, jug, sugar basin, spoons, knives and forks and dishes – by a choice little collection of old silver, in fact, that Mr Balham had recently inherited from a great-aunt.

After ringing up the police and arranging, as he thought, for them to rescue him from the hands of the villain in the nick of time, William had set out for Mr Balham's house. There, he had effected an entry by means of a drain-pipe and an open bedroom window, and had begun a systematic search for the confidential documents. A thorough examination of Mr Balham's bedroom had revealed nothing (though on visiting it later in the evening that mild man was to use language that would almost certainly have induced his great-aunt to alter her will), and so William had crept cautiously and silently downstairs and started on the dining-room. The sideboard cupboard had seemed a likely hiding-place and, finding it full of silver, William had taken it out piece by piece in order to make sure that the confidential documents were not hidden among them. It was at this moment that Mr Balham and the policeman entered. They stood and stared at him in silence.

Then the policeman said to Mr Balham, 'That your boy?'

'No,' said the amazed Mr Balham. 'Never seen him before.'

William looked sternly at the policeman.

'You've come a bit too soon,' he said. The policeman looked down at him.

'Yes,' he said drily, 'I can see I have.'

'I've not found anythin' yet,' said William.

IT WAS AT THIS MOMENT THAT MR BALHAM AND THE
POLICEMAN ENTERED.

The policeman looked down at the silver.

'You don't seem to have done so badly,' he said.

'The only things of value in the house,' said Mr
Balham.

'Oh yes, he knew what to come for, all right,' said the
policeman. 'A proper haul he'd got, too. Or would have had

if I hadn't come along . . . I don't know who you're working with, my lad, but whoever it is has given you away. We
had a telephone call asking us to come along and nab you.'

'*Me?*' said William in amazement. 'It wasn't to nab me
– it was to nab *him*.' He pointed to Mr Balham who was
gazing down at him sadly. '*He's* the one you've gotter nab.'

'That's a good one!' chuckled the policeman.

'Juvenile crime!' said Mr Balham, shaking his head
mournfully. 'I've heard a lot about it, but I little thought to
have it brought home to me like this. Why, he's a mere
child!'

'Lucky for us we got that call,' said the policeman.
'Ten to one he'd have got away with it if we hadn't. Yes,
young feller-me-lad, if someone hadn't rung us up and
told us to come along here—'

'It was *me* rang you up,' said William. 'I tell you, it's
him you've gotter get hold of. He's the crim'nal, not me.
Look!'

Before either of them could stop him, he had caught
hold of Mr Balham's moustache and pulled it as hard as
he could.

Mr Balham gave a yell of anguish.

'Assault!' he said, nursing his face tenderly in both
hands. 'Add assault to your charge, constable. Theft and
assault. And I hope the magistrate won't be lenient.'

'He's got it stuck on jolly fast,' said William, 'or else he's grown it. I bet that's it. He's grown it . . . But it's a disguise, all right.'

The policeman took out his notebook.

'I want your name and address, my lad,' he said, 'and an explanation of what you're doing with that silver.'

'*Me?*' said William indignantly. 'Look here! You don't understand. It's not me what's the criminal. It's *him*. He's ole Grissel. He's handin' the country over to ole Hitler. I tell you, I've *seen* him doin' it. He was doin' it all this mornin'. *Listen*. If you let him go now he'll give the country over to ole Hitler straight away. I tell you I've *heard* him doin' it – telephonin' people an' tellin' 'em that the whole place was blown up jus' to scare 'em. He's got people workin' under him, too, same as he had in Norfolk. They were all telephonin' an' tellin' people the whole place was blown up jus' to scare 'em. They said that Marleigh police station was blown up. Well, that's a lie 'cause I passed it. An' Pithurst Lane an' Hill Road an—'

A light was slowly dawning in Mr Balham's mind.

'Wait a minute, wait a minute,' he said, giving his injured lip a reassuring final caress. 'Where were you this morning when you heard all this?'

*

William walked slowly down the road homeward. Mr Balham was an extremely patriotic little man, and he felt that William's zeal, though mistaken, was on the whole commendable. After dismissing the policeman, he had refreshed William with a large currant bun and a glass of lemonade and finally presented him with half a crown. Against his will, William had been persuaded of the innocence of his host. He was reluctant to abandon the carefully built-up case against him, but the currant bun and lemonade and half-crown consoled him. He decided to buy some new arrows with the half-crown. All his old ones, having found unauthorised marks of one sort or another, had been confiscated. He would go to the field behind the old barn with the Outlaws tomorrow morning, and they would have a bow-and-arrow practice. It was a long time since they'd had a bow-and-arrow practice. When he reached home, he found his mother still at work on the table napkins.

'Well, dear,' she said, looking up from her work, 'had a nice afternoon?'

'Yes thanks,' said William absently, wondering whether it wouldn't be better, after all, to buy water-pistols.

'What have you been doing?' went on Mrs Brown.

William drew his mind with an effort from the all-important question of the half-crown (he must not decide in too much of a hurry; he could do with another boat; it was some time since they had had a regatta on the stream) to the details of an afternoon that was already vanishing into the mists of the past.

'Me?' he said vaguely. 'This afternoon? Nothin' much. I caught that man you were all talkin' about this mornin', an' I was arrested for stealin' silver an' someone gave me half a crown.'

Mrs Brown was accustomed to her son's fantastic imaginary adventures.

'Yes, I'm sure you did, dear,' she said. 'Will you pass me the scissors?'

CHAPTER 3

WILLIAM – THE FIRE-FIGHTER

WILLIAM and the Outlaws were thrilled to find that an A.F.S. 'area' had sprung up overnight in Hadley. At least, it wasn't there when they went into Hadley one week, and it was there the next. It appeared suddenly in a garage on the outskirts of the town, complete with trailers, pumps, and a heterogeneous collection of cars. Added to this were miles of hose-pipe and a glorious spate of water. All behind an imposing erection of sandbags.

The Outlaws could not tear themselves away from the fascinating spectacle. God-like beings in long rubber boots reaching almost to their waists waded about the swimming garage floor, polished the trailers, tinkered with the cars and did physical jerks. Occasionally they sallied forth with cars and trailers to neighbouring ponds, where they detached the trailers, unwound the hoses, and sent breath-taking sprays of water in every direction.

Forgotten were all the other interests which had once filled the Outlaws' lives. They now went down to Hadley

Garage immediately after breakfast and stayed there till it was time to go home for lunch, returning immediately afterwards to stay there till tea-time. A house at the back of the garage was used as cook-house, dining-room and dormitory. Savoury smells came from it. Roars of laughter came from the dining-room when the god-like beings assembled there for meals.

At first the Outlaws contented themselves with watching this paradise through the gates. Then, cautiously, they entered and hung about just inside. Nothing happened. No one took any notice of them.

It was William who first dared to give a hand with a trailer that a small man with a black moustache was cleaning. The small man seemed to accept his presence and his help as a matter of course, even addressing him as 'mate', which made William feel dizzy with rapture. The other Outlaws followed . . . No one objected to them. Some of the men even seemed pleased to dally in their work to talk to them and explain the various contraptions to them. One of them let William hold a hose-pipe.

'I don't see why we sh'u'nt join 'em prop'ly,' said William to the Outlaws as they went home, drunk with pride. 'Well, we *helped*, din' we? I bet we'd be jolly useful to 'm. I don't see why we sh'u'nt join prop'ly.'

'We've not got uniforms,' Ginger reminded him.

William dismissed this objection with a sweeping gesture.

'They don't matter. Anyway, they've only got those A.F.S. letters on ordin'ry suits. We could easy get a bit of red cotton an' put A.F.S. on ours.'

'I bet they wouldn't let us join,' said Henry.

'Well, we needn't 'zactly ask 'em,' said William. 'We'll jus' go same as we did today, an' do a bit of helpin', and they'll get used to us gradual till they won't know we weren't part of 'em right at the start.'

The others continued to look doubtful.

'The little one was jolly nice to us,' went on William. 'I bet they'll all be nice to us once they get to know us.'

'I've known people not be,' Douglas reminded him.

'I bet these will be,' said William, the optimist. 'I bet they'll be jolly grateful to us. Anyway, I vote we jus' go an' join 'em tomorrow an' do all the things they do. We'll have badges same as them an' I bet they'll think we've been part of 'em all along. We'll make the badges of red cotton—'

'We've not got any red cotton,' said Douglas.

'Well, we can get some, can't we?' said William irritably. 'Goodness me! You all go on an' *on* makin' objections. I bet I find some in Ethel's work-box. She's got every poss'ble colour of cotton there is . . . Anyway,' firmly, 'we're part of the A.F.S. now, an' we'll go there tomorrow morning an' do all the things they do . . . I'll go'n' have a look for the red cotton now.'

He found the red cotton (or rather silk) by the simple process of turning out the contents of Ethel's work-box on to her bedroom floor and rummaging among them till he found it. Then conscientiously he bundled everything back and was much aggrieved by Ethel's reproaches later in the day.

'Well, I put 'em *back,* din' I?' he said. 'Well, they looked all right to me . . . I put 'em *back.* Well, I'd *gotter* have that red cotton . . . No, I can't tell you why . . . It's somethin' to do with winnin' the war . . . No, I can't tell you what it is . . . The Gov'ment says we mustn't go talkin' about things we're doin' to win the war. You don't know where ole Hitler is, listenin'.'

He took the reel of red silk to the old barn and also a needle that he had thoughtfully purloined at the same time.

'It'll be quite easy,' he said. 'You jus' sew A.F.S. on, an' I bet it'll look same as theirs.'

A few moments later he doubtfully surveyed the spidery network of red threads that he had made on his coat.

'Well, anyway,' he said, 'you can see it's meant to be A.F.S. if you look close enough. It's a jolly good A and the F's not bad, an' I bet the S doesn't matter so much. Well, stands to reason you can't do a letter like S with an ordin'ry needle. I bet they have special ones.'

With frowning concentration each of the others out-lined spidery hieroglyphics on his coat. They, too, inspected the finished results doubtfully – results more suggestive of laundry marks gone mad than a badge of Government service.

'They're not bad,' said William. 'They're red, anyway, an' it doesn't matter what the 'zact letters are. Well, we'll be with the real ones, so people'll know it's meant to be A.F.S.'

Wishing to give an impression of good discipline, he marched his band through the main street of Hadley the next morning and then boldly in through the garage gates. It happened that the A.F.S. was drawn up for parade. They stood stiffly in a row, their backs to the gate, waiting for the Section Officer to appear through the door of what had once been the motor sale-room.

William marched his band up to the end of the line, where they took their places, standing straight to atten-tion. At that moment the Section Officer appeared at the doorway. His eyes swept down the ranks of the men to rest finally upon the Outlaws . . . His face darkened. He was a youthful platinum blond, with an exaggerated idea of his own importance. He couldn't tolerate anything that made him appear ridiculous, and he considered that

WILLIAM HAD MARCHED HIS BAND UP TO THE END OF THE
LINE, WHERE THEY TOOK THEIR PLACES, STANDING
STRAIGHT TO ATTENTION.

the presence of the Outlaws at his firemen parade made
him appear ridiculous.

He bore down on them furiously.

'Get out of this at once!' he thundered. 'How dare you
come in here! Don't you know that you're trespassing?'

'Yes, but—' began William.

'GET OUT OF THIS AT ONCE!' THUNDERED THE SECTION
OFFICER. 'HOW DARE YOU COME IN HERE! DON'T YOU
KNOW THAT YOU'RE TRESPASSING?'

The Section Officer was large and muscular and he
looked like business.

'Al' right,' muttered William hastily, and withdrew
with his Outlaws in as good order as possible.

Outside he turned to them.

'Well, I like that!' he said indignantly. 'I jolly well *like*

85

that. I bet he's no right to go turnin' people out of the A.F.S. I bet he'd jolly well get into trouble if the King knew that he was goin' about turnin' people out of the A.F.S. I've a good mind to write and tell him—'

'When we've took all that trouble over our badges, too,' said Ginger gloomily, looking down at the vague and spidery red threads that adorned his coat.

'Let's wait till he's done an' then go in again,' suggested Henry.

William shook his head. Despite his youth he was not without judgement and had spent many years of his short life gauging how far one could go with grown-ups of various types. He judged – quite rightly – that, for the present at any rate, it wasn't safe to go any further with that particular young man.

'No, let's go home,' he said. 'I'm sick of the rotten old A.F.S. Let's go'n' play Red Indians—'

They went home and played Red Indians, but somehow all the glamour had faded from the game. None of them could put any conviction into it. It wasn't real any longer. Only the A.F.S. was real.

'Tell you what,' said William finally. 'We can go'n' watch 'em same as we used to . . . We can do that, at any rate. He can't stop us goin' to watch 'em same as we used to . . . An' we'll keep our badges. He can't stop us havin' badges . . . They might all fall ill sudden or get burnt up in a fire, an' then I bet they'd be jolly glad to have us.'

They went down to Hadley the next morning and took up their old position outside the A.F.S. station, their noses glued as usual to the bars of the gate. But evidently not even that was to be allowed them. Section Officer Perkins espied them, recognised them, and bore down on them, his face flushed with the memory of yesterday's affront to his dignity and with secret apprehension of another.

'Clear off at once, you boys!' he said. 'I won't have you hanging about like this. If I find you here again, I'll hand you over to the police.'

Reluctantly, the Outlaws drifted away.

'Well,' said William with rising indignation. 'I like that. I jolly well *like* that. The street's not his, is it? The whole place isn't his, is it? Who does he think he is? Lord Mayor of London or Hitler or what? Let's go back there. Gosh! He can't stop people *lookin'* at him, can he? He'll have to make himself invisible if he's goin' to stop people *lookin'* at him. Crumbs! That's a new lor, that is, that people aren't allowed to *look* at people . . . I bet there'll be a jolly lot of accidents,' he went on sarcastically, 'with people runnin' into each other an' suchlike now people aren't allowed to *look* at each other . . . Corks! That's a jolly funny lor, that is!'

'Let's go back there, then,' said Ginger.

But William was reluctant to go back. It wasn't a question of the law. Grown-ups, as William had learnt by bitter experience, were a law to themselves. William was a brave boy, but not one to court disaster unnecessarily.

''S no good,' he said gloomily. 'He'd only come an' make us go away again. I've met people like him before. Tyrunts same as the ones in hist'ry. Ole Stinks at school's one. Well, come to that, all schoolmasters are. They're all tyrunts, same as the ones in hist'ry. An' this ole Section Officer's another. I shouldn't be surprised if he's a schoolmaster in disguise. You can't mistake 'em, but – well, I'm not goin' back there. I 'spect he wishes we would. I 'spect he'd jolly well like us to, but I'm not goin' to . . . Tell you what . . .' A gleam of inspiration flashed into his face. '*Tell* you what. We'll have one of our own. Well, he can't stop us doin' that, can he? He can stop us joinin' his, but he can't stop us havin' one of our own. We'll have a sep'rate branch, an' I bet we put out more fires than what his does.'

'It'll be a bit difficult, won't it?' said Ginger thoughtfully.

'Course it won't,' said William stoutly.

'We've not got a trailer nor a hose-pipe nor anythin',' said Douglas.

'Corks!' groaned William. 'You can't do anythin' but make objections. I never saw anythin' like you. We c'n get a wheelbarrow – can't we? – an' a hose from the garden an' we've got our badges an' that's all we need. We'll do all the same sort of things they do, an' we'll know when there's a fire 'cause we'll see them goin' to it, an' we can go along an' help, an' I bet we can put out fires as well as what they can – or a jolly sight better. You only need *water* for puttin' out fires an' water's cheap enough, isn't it? An' there's no *lor* to stop anyone what wants to puttin' out a fire, is there?'

His eloquence was, as ever, convincing, and the Outlaws gradually found themselves becoming convinced.

'We've gotter have a place to be an A.F.S. in,' objected Henry feebly, 'an' the ole barn's too far away. We sh'u'n't know what they were doin'.'

'Course we can't use the ole barn,' said William. 'It's miles away. We've gotter stay joined to the A.F.S. here. We're *part* of the A.F.S. here, whether ole Monkey-face wants us to be or not. I bet he'll be jolly glad of us before we've finished.'

'Yes, but what about a place?' persisted Henry.

'There's that bit of empty ground nex' the garage,' said William. 'That'll do for us, all right.'

There was, indeed, a small plot of waste ground next the garage and on this the Outlaws took up their position the next morning. They had a wheelbarrow in which was a bucket of water, a length of hose and a garden syringe that Henry had 'borrowed' from the tool shed.

It was of an up-to-date kind and had a little contraption at the end of a length of tubing that you dropped into the bucket of water and that enabled you to spray out the whole of its contents without dipping the nozzle into the water. The gardener, the apple of whose eye it was, had been called up recently, and Henry was hoping for the best.

'I'll get into an awful row, though, if my father finds out,' he said.

'Well, *goodness*!' said William, indignantly. 'You'd think that winnin' the war came before squirtin' a few roses an' suchlike, wouldn't you? Well, it seems a bit more important to *me*, anyway. Funny thing to think squirtin' a few roses more important than winnin' the war. I bet your father could get put in prison for thinkin' that.'

'Oh, well,' said Henry mildly, 'he's jolly busy jus' now so p'raps it'll be all right. What'll we do first?'

'We'll see what they're doin' an' do that,' said William. 'Go'n' see what they're doin', Ginger.'

Ginger went to peep through the gates of the garage.

'They're doin' drill,' he said when he returned. 'Ole Monkey-face is drillin' 'em.'

'All right,' said William. 'We'll drill too.'

For the rest of the morning, William's band of A.F.S. followed the procedure of the mother branch next door. Ginger was sent round at frequent intervals to report any change in the programme.

'They're cleanin' the trailers now.'

And at once the Outlaws set to work upon the wheelbarrow, turning it upside down and dusting it with handkerchiefs already so grubby from various other activities that a little dirt more or less made no difference.

'They're squirtin' their hose now.'

And at once the Outlaws took down the bucket of water and set to work with the garden syringe. Fortunately it was only a short walk out of the town to refill the bucket at a convenient roadside ditch.

Passers-by looked with amusement at the four boys busily intent on imitating their neighbours, but the Outlaws were too much occupied to have any time to spare for passers-by . . . If Section Officer Perkins knew of this caricature of his dignified proceedings taking place on the other side of the garage wall, he gave no signs of it. His face still wore its expression of portentous self-importance.

At the end of the day William was well satisfied with the progress made by his band.

'We've done all the things they've done,' he said, 'An' we've done 'em jus' as well – or a jolly sight better. We'll come again tomorrow, an' I bet we'll soon be beatin' 'em hollow.'

Their ardour was unabated next morning, and they took up their position on the piece of waste ground.

'P'raps they'll be doin' somethin' a bit different today,' said William hopefully.

Ginger, sent to reconnoitre, brought news that they were preparing to fix trailers on to the cars.

'They're goin' out somewhere,' he said. 'I bet they're goin' up to Lengham ponds.'

'All right,' said William, in his most business-like manner, 'we'll go there, too. Get everything ready quick.'

In a few moments the A.F.S. cars came out of the garage, occupied by Section Officer Perkins and his band, the trailers attached.

At once William and his company emerged from the piece of waste land, wheeling the wheelbarrow, complete with bucket of water, length of hose and syringe. Section Officer Perkins turned to glare at them, then drove on furiously.

'Well, of course,' said William as the cars vanished into the distance, 'we can't keep up with them. We're not *tryin'* to keep up with them. But I bet they're goin' to Lengham ponds. We'll go there anyway an' see.'

They trundled their way through the town, spilling a

good deal of water and rousing much amusement among the onlookers.

'Bet they're at Lengham ponds,' William kept saying.

And there, sure enough, they were. They were putting one end of a hose into the pond and directing water from the other end at various spots indicated by Section Officer Perkins. As the Outlaws appeared, they were just beginning to pack up the trailers to return home.

The Outlaws trundled their barrow down to the pond, took out their syringe, and, under William's direction, squirted a thin stream of water at the A.F.S.'s latest target, a tall, thin birch tree on the edge of the pond. It was, perhaps, unfortunate that Section Officer Perkins happened to be passing behind the birch tree.

The thin stream of water hit him full in the eye as he turned round . . . He strode towards the Outlaws, his face white with anger, and William, realising the inadequacy of his forces to deal with the situation, led a hasty retreat into the surrounding wood.

'He's jealous, that's what he is,' he said, as, having watched the departure of the rival band, he returned to the wheelbarrow, still carrying the precious syringe. 'He's jealous 'cause we're as good as what his lot are.'

'He was mad 'cause that water hit him in the eye,' said Ginger, putting the facts of the case more simply.

'Well, goodness me!' said William. 'Fancy a fireman mindin' a bit of water in his eye. Corks! A fireman's gotter get used to bein' *soaked* all over. Jus' shows what a rotten fireman he is,' he ended with satisfaction. 'I *knew* he was a rotten fireman soon as I saw him. Anyone'd be a rotten fireman with hair that colour. Stands to reason.'

The routine of drilling and cleaning the wheelbarrow soon began to pall, and William's plans of emulating the canteen by making a fire on the piece of waste land and cooking a mixture of cold sausage and roly-poly pudding (purloined from the larder) in an old saucepan (purloined from the dustbin) was nipped in the bud by a passing policeman.

To make matters worse, Section Officer Perkins developed a new technique. He came and watched the Outlaws with a sneer of superior amusement. He brought his friends to sneer at them. He once deliberately directed the hose over the wall of the garage so that William was soaked from head to foot. Fortunately, William's mother was out when he reached home, and his vague explanation, given on her return, of having 'got into a bit of water' was accepted with the inevitable, 'William, you are dreadful! What *will* you do next?'

'What we've gotter do,' said William, addressing his band

the following morning, 'is to find a fire 'fore they do, an' put it out. *That'll* show 'em, all right. They'll treat us a bit diff'rent after *that*. Jolly snooks for them, comin' along after we've put the fire out. Come on. Let's go an' have a look for a fire.'

Refilling the bucket at the ditch, testing the syringe to make sure that it was in working order, giving the wheel-barrow a final dust over with their handkerchiefs, the Outlaw A.F.S. sallied forth in search of a fire.

They went through the main streets of Hadley, inspecting each house and shop carefully, without result.

'Gosh!' said William at last, irritably. 'You'd think with all these people there'd be a fire *somewhere*. To see 'em throwin' down matches an' cigarette ends all over the place you'd think there'd be no end of fires. Can't think what *happens* to 'em all.'

They abandoned the main streets at last and began to roam the smaller back streets, still inspecting each house carefully for signs of a conflagration.

'Wouldn't do 'em any harm to let us have a little one,' he muttered pathetically. '*Mean*, I call it.'

'Well, they don't *want* fires,' Ginger reminded him mildly.

'No, but – well, you wouldn't think a *little* one'd do 'em any harm. I mean, when you read of all the fires there are in the newspapers it seems sort of *mean* of 'em to start bein' careful just when we're lookin' for one.'

'S'pose we couldn't start one ourselves,' suggested Douglas.

William shook his head.

'No,' he said reluctantly. 'That wouldn't count. We've gotter find one.'

'Look!' said Ginger excitedly, pointing to a small back window. It was open a few inches at the top, and from the opening swirls of white vapour were pouring out.

'That's smoke! That's a fire!'

William stopped, set down the wheelbarrow and looked at it with the air of an expert.

'Yes, that's a fire all right,' he said.

He advanced and made a closer inspection through the window. Nothing could be seen but the thick eddies of white vapour.

'It's cert'nly a fire all right,' he said again.

The four Outlaws stood gazing in at the window.

'Can't see any flame,' said Henry.

'Course you can't,' said William. 'It's right inside the house, the flame is. We've gotter fight our way through the smoke to the flame. We've gotter tie handkerchiefs over our mouths an' fight our way through the smoke same as the real ones do. There's probably people unconscious inside, overpowered by the fumes, same as there are in the newspapers, an' we've gotter rescue 'em.'

'Won't we let the others help at all?' said Ginger, somewhat appalled by the magnitude of the task that lay before them.

'Oh, yes, we'll send 'em a message about it,' said William, 'an' we'll let 'em come along an' help, but we'll start on it alone first jus' to *show* 'em. We'll prob'ly 've put it out an' rescued all the people by the time they get here.'

A small boy in spectacles was passing along the street. William called to him.

'I say,' he said. 'Go'n' tell the A.F.S. at Hadley Garage that there's a fire at,' he glanced at the number of the street, 'ten, Nelson Street, and tell 'em to come quick.'

'A' right,' said the boy, and he set off with unexpected agility in the direction of the garage.

'Now we've gotter put wet handkerchiefs over our faces,' said William, 'an' get the syringe thing full and then fight our way in through the smoke. Ginger 'n' me'll put out the fire, an' Henry an' Douglas can rescue the people. I 'spect they'll be unconscious. I 'spect you'll have to squirt water on 'em and drag 'em out . . . It's jolly dangerous an' I 'spect that other lot of A.F.S.'ll get here too late to help. I 'spec we'll get medals or somethin'.'

It took longer than they thought to adjust the wet

handkerchiefs. At last they were ready, however, and, armed with syringe and pail of water, headed by William, they marched up to the door.

William flung it open.

Clouds of white vapour enveloped him. Almost at the same time a door into the room from the house side opened and the figure of a woman entered. They could see it dimly through the thick vapour. Ginger pointed the syringe at it and squirted. He explained afterwards that his whole mind was set on squirting and somehow he couldn't help squirting at the first thing he saw move.

The woman gave a loud scream. It was a scream of anger and indignation. It was definitely not the grateful scream of someone being rescued from a fire. Instinctively the Outlaws drew back, and at that moment the A.F.S. from Hadley Garage arrived. The messenger had been a fleeter runner than he looked and had met them at the gate just starting out, completely equipped, for a mobility exercise. They had driven straight to the address given them by the spectacled small boy. Section Officer Perkins appeared at the door. Behind him was a fireman holding the nozzle of a hose, the other end of which was being attached to the nearest hydrant.

With the opening of the door the atmosphere was gradually clearing. It showed a kettle boiling vigorously on a gas ring. It showed a large woman, standing arms akimbo and glaring angrily at Section Officer Perkins. Her face was dripping with water from Ginger's syringe, but somehow that did not detract from the awful impressiveness of her appearance.

'How *dare* you!' she thundered.

'I – I beg your pardon,' stammered Section Officer Perkin's.

'I said "How *dare* you!"'

'I – I – I don't know what you mean!' spluttered Section Officer Perkins. 'I – I—'

'I shall report you to headquarters,' went on the woman. 'As if I hadn't got enough trouble today. First that girl puts the kettle on and forgets all about it for over half an hour.' She turned and switched off the gas with a sudden vicious gesture. 'Gas bills mean nothing to *her* . . . And then you and your lot come larking along. Let me tell you, young man, I can take a joke as well as anyone, but I don't call this a joke. I've heard of your sort and I think it's time a stop was put to it. You've chosen the wrong house to come to with your tom-fool tricks and I shall report you to headquarters this minute. Larking into respectable folks' houses and turning your hose-pipes on to them.'

'I – I never turned the hose-pipe on to you,' protested the Section Officer indignantly.

'Am I wet or am I not?' demanded the woman, turning her portly person to him for his inspection. There wasn't any doubt at all that she was wet. Her hair was wet, her face was wet, her ample bosom was wet. 'And,' she went on without waiting for his answer, 'you've got the impudence to say you never turned the hose-pipe on me.'

'I – I – I never did!' said Section Officer Perkins again.

'Funny thing, isn't it?' she said sarcastically.

The steam had now mostly found its way out or hung in beads of moisture on the walls and ceiling of the little spick-and-span scullery. 'Funny thing to come in here, and get a squirt of water in my face and then look round and find you standing there with your hose-pipe. You ought to be ashamed of yourself. A man of your age larking about like a schoolboy! You deserve the sack and I hope you get it.'

'Madam,' said the Section Officer desperately, aware of his firemen sniggering behind him, 'I protest. I got a message that there was a fire here and I came along.'

'That's a nice tale,' said the woman. 'Who sent the message and why need you start squirting me in the face the minute you get here?'

Section Officer Perkins looked round. There was no one there but his own A.F.S. squad. William had long ago quietly withdrawn his band under cover of the steam before anyone had realised their presence.

'I can't understand what happened,' he said. 'A boy brought a message that there was a fire here and we were needed at once, and, as for turning on the hose, the very idea's ridiculous.'

'So *you* say,' said the woman darkly. 'I prefer to believe my eyes. And now that's enough of your sauce, young man. Off you go or you won't be the only one throwing water in people's faces. Off you go and take your grinning monkeys with you. I've got work to do if you haven't.'

With that she pushed him back and slammed the door in his face. Section Officer Perkins drove slowly back to his station. His face was set and stern. He looked like an extremely dignified young man whose dignity has been sorely affronted. As he passed the piece of waste ground next to the garage he drove very slowly indeed, fixing his gaze intently on William and the Outlaws. They were, however, engaged on the innocent task of cleaning the wheelbarrow with the air of having been hard at work on it all morning.

Section Officer Perkins went into his office looking thoughtful.

As soon as the A.F.S. had disappeared through the garage gates, William laid aside the handkerchief, with which he had been making a pretence of polishing the wheels, and heaved a sigh of relief.

'*That's* all right,' he said. 'Gosh! I was afraid they'd
've found out. Well, goodness me! It wasn't our fault. It
looked like a fire. How was anyone to *know?* I bet
they'd 've thought it was a fire all right. I bet *they'd* 've
squirted her, too . . . Corks! Wasn't she mad! It was a
jolly good thing there was all that mist about so's they
didn't see us.'

'Wouldn't he be mad if he knew!' chuckled Ginger.

'Yes,' said Douglas, 'but he's not likely to find out now.'

But they were wrong. Section Officer Perkins had
already found out. Chance had most unkindly delivered
the Outlaws into his hand. He was going out to a neighbouring shop for some cigarettes when it happened. He
met the small boy who had taken William's message
coming out of a sweet shop.

Questioned, he gave a clear and concise account of the
circumstances in which he had been sent to summon the
A.F.S. to the 'fire'. He described William and the Outlaws
and their fire-fighting equipment in a way that left no
room for doubt.

Section Officer Perkins bore down upon the Outlaws
just as they were setting out for home. There was a grimly
triumphant gleam in his eye. He had made further
inquiries since meeting the small boy and had come prepared to give a knock-out blow to his enemies.

They listened with impassive faces and silent dismay to his short but pointed speech. He had discovered, he said, that it was they who had played the 'disgraceful trick' on him this morning, sending for him to a fire, when they knew perfectly well that there was no fire at all. He had got all their names and addresses and was going to see the father of each of them that evening. He hoped they would be severely punished. If ever he caught them on that piece of waste ground again he would send for the police . . . Then he swung on his heel and went away, smiling to himself. The Outlaws stared after him.

'Corks!' said William at last.

'Crumbs!' said Ginger.

'Gosh!' said Douglas and Henry simultaneously.

'My father'll be mad,' said Ginger. 'He'll never b'lieve we weren't playing a trick on 'em.'

'Neither will mine,' agreed the other Outlaws gloomily.

'We're goin' to get in an awful row,' said William. ''S never any good tellin' my father what really happened. He won't even listen.'

'Neither will mine,' agreed the other Outlaws.

'I shan't mind not comin' here again,' said William. 'I was gettin' tired of it, anyway. I'm sick of jus' drillin' an' dustin' the wheelbarrow – I mean the trailer – an' that's all they seem to do. I've jolly well had enough of it, an' I'd 've stopped tomorrow anyway, but – corks! I'm goin' to have an awful time! My father was mad last night 'cause an old woman came tellin' tales about me breakin' her cucumber frame. I was only tryin' to hit a tree with a stone. I didn't *mean* it to go in her old cucumber frame. Gosh! You should've heard the way he went on at me. He said he was sick of people complainin' an' the nex' time it happened he'd give me somethin' to remember an' I bet he jolly well will, too. He's got an awful temper.'

Gloomily the Outlaws all agreed that their fathers had awful tempers, too.

'D'you think if we went to him and explained . . .' said Ginger.

'No, not him!' said William, who was on the whole a fairly good judge of human nature. 'He wouldn't b'lieve us, anyway, an' he'd jus' enjoy bein' nasty.'

'If we said we were sorry . . .' said Henry tentatively.

'He'd enjoy that still more,' said William, 'an' he'll go'n' complain to our fathers jus' the same whatever we do.'

'I'd jolly well like to give him somethin' to complain of,' said Ginger bitterly.

William looked thoughtful for a few moments, then said slowly:

'Yes . . . that wouldn't be a bad idea . . . That wouldn't

be a bad idea at all . . . If I've gotter get into a row I'd rather get into it for doin' somethin' worth doin'. My father couldn't be worse than he's goin' to be, anyway, an' I'd like to do somethin' to get even with old Monkey-face.'

The Outlaws brightened. Better go down with colours flying . . . Better strike a blow at the enemy before yielding to superior force.

'What can we do?' said Douglas.

'Well, that's what we've gotter think out,' said William.

A new animation possessed the little band. Secretly each had been growing bored with such limited scope as their A.F.S. activities allowed them, and welcomed the wider field afforded by a plan of revenge.

'We've gotter find out somethin' about him first,' said William. 'Where he lives an' suchlike. When I have a revenge I like to take a bit of trouble over it. I'm jolly good at revenges,' he ended modestly.

'We'll all have a good think,' said Ginger. 'Anyway, it's nearly one o'clock now an' we'd better go home. 'S no good getting into any more rows. We've all got a jolly big one comin' tonight, anyway.'

'A'right,' said William. 'We'll meet in the ole barn after lunch. Let's all have a jolly good think while we're havin' lunch . . . Hope it's jam roly-poly. I can think better on jam roly-poly than on rice puddin'.'

They met in the old barn soon after two o'clock. By a lucky chance Henry's family had been discussing Section Officer Perkins during lunch and he came primed with news of him.

'He lives at that house called Green Gates jus' outside Hadley an' he's not married—'

''Spect he is, an' murdered her,' put in William darkly.

'An' he's got a housekeeper, but she's had to go home to look after her father what's ill an' he was askin' Mrs Monks if she knew of another an' she said she'd try'n' find him one. He's jus' got a char in the mornings now.'

''Spect he murdered that housekeeper,' said William. 'He'd've murdered us soon as look at us.'

'Well, what're we goin' to do to him?' said Ginger.

'Have our revenge on him,' said William.

'Yes, but how?'

'Well, it wasn't jam roly-poly,' said William, 'but I got a sort of idea.'

'What was it?' said Douglas.

'Suet pudding'n' syrup. Better than rice puddin' anyway.'

'No, I meant the idea.'

'Oh, yes,' said William. 'Well, it's gotter be somethin' to do with the A.F.S. Somethin' to do with a hose or water or somethin'.'

'We've not got a hose,' said Henry, 'an' if we squirted him with a syringe we'd get in a worse row than ever.'

'I was wond'rin' about the bucket of water,' said William.

'What about it?'

'I was wond'rin' if we could fix it up over a door so's it fell down soon as he opened it. I've read of people doin' that. It'd be a jolly good revenge.'

The Outlaws considered the idea with interest. There was something of poetic justice in it that appealed to them. Section Officer Perkins had got them into trouble over water. It was only fair that he should get into trouble himself over water. It would be a glorious and fitting end to the Outlaws' branch of the A.F.S. thus thoroughly to douse the man who had brought about its end.

'Might be difficult to fix up,' said Douglas dubiously.

'We can try, anyway,' said William. 'We can have a jolly good try. I bet it won't be difficult.'

'Well, he's bein' down at the garage all this afternoon,' said Henry. 'I found out that. That'll give us time.'

'We'll have to be careful,' said Douglas.

'Oh, we'll be careful all right,' said William carelessly. 'Corks! When I think of him goin' into that room an' the bucket of water fallin' right over his head . . .'

He chuckled. As usual, he saw the scheme in its finished perfection, magnificently ignoring the intervening details.

107

Again Douglas looked doubtfully at the bucket.

'It's jolly heavy to carry full of water,' he said. 'I dunno how we're goin' to get it fixed up on top of a door.'

'Oh, we'll find a way,' said William. 'First thing to do is to get it to the house . . . We'll get it there, an' then we'll find a way to fix it up all right. Come on . . . 'S time we started.'

They filled the bucket with water and carried it in turn across the fields to the outskirts of Hadley. As each one took the weight of the bucket he felt secret doubts about the success of the scheme, but William's glorious optimism swept them along with it.

'We c'n stand on a chair,' he said vaguely. 'We'll fix it up all right, once we get it there. I bet it'll be easy fixin' it up, once we get it there.'

They approached Green Gates cautiously from the back, making their way into the garden – a neat little garden with an ornamental pond – by way of the hedge and sending Ginger on in front to spy out the land.

''S empty all right,' he said when he returned. 'There's no one in it. An' there's a room full of steam same as there was in that cottage this mornin'. He must've left a kettle on, too.'

Still carrying the bucket, they approached nearer. William put down the bucket and stared in at a downstairs window through clouds of eddying smoke.

'Gosh! This *is* a fire, all right,' he said. 'I can see flames. G'n' ring up the fire station, Henry,' he went on, 'an' I bet we put it out before they come.'

He flung up the window and carefully lifted himself and the bucket of water into the room, then flung the water in the direction of the flame. There was a sizzling sound.

'Good!' said William, half choked with smoke. 'Get some more water from the pond.'

Ginger filled the bucket there and handed it to William through the window. Douglas fought his way into the kitchen and finding another bucket there, filled it at the tap. Gradually the flames died down, leaving a large hole burnt in the carpet, the walls and ceilings blackened.

At that moment the fire brigade arrived. The Outlaws, their faces blackened almost beyond recognition, received them proudly.

'We've put it out,' they said.

The captain entered and looked round the waterlogged room.

'It wasn't *much* of a fire, of course,' said William modestly, 'but it cert'nly was a fire.'

'Yes, it certainly was a fire,' agreed the captain. His practised eye fell on the groove burnt on the table obviously by a lighted cigarette before it fell on to the carpet.

AT THAT MOMENT THE A.F.S. ARRIVED, HEADED BY
SECTION OFFICER PERKINS.

At that moment the A.F.S. arrived, headed by Section
Officer Perkins, looking white and tense. The captain met
him at the door.

'Well, Perkins,' he said with rather a malicious smile,
'you're just too late. So were we, as a matter of fact . . .
You left a lighted cigarette on the table, didn't you?'

'WELL, PERKINS,' SAID THE CAPTAIN WITH RATHER A
MALICIOUS SMILE, 'YOU'RE JUST TOO LATE.'

'Y – y – yes,' stammered Section Officer Perkins. 'I – I
remembered as soon as the call came through. The telephone went and I put down my cigarette to answer it and
then someone came round with a car to give me a lift to
the garage and I quite forgot about the cigarette and—'

'Well, you've got these plucky boys to thank for putting it out,' said the captain, waving his hand towards the
blackened Outlaws.

Section Officer Perkins turned to the blackened Outlaws, recognised them slowly through their coating of
grime, and stared at them as though he couldn't believe
his eyes. His mouth dropped open. He looked like a man
in the throes of a nightmare. He gasped and gulped.

'W – w – what happened?' he said at last.

'They saw the fire,' said the captain, 'and very pluckily
came in and put it out. They telephoned us as well.
They've shown great pluck and presence of mind, and I
think you ought to be very grateful to them.'

'Y – y – yes,' stammered Section Officer Perkins. 'Yes,
of course, I am.'

'A very dangerous habit, leaving lighted cigarettes
about,' said the captain. He had always disliked Section
Officer Perkins and was enjoying his discomfiture.

'Y – y – yes,' stammered Section Officer Perkins.

He was still staring at the four Outlaws in the manner of
a fascinated rabbit, as if he could never take his eyes off
them again. If he hadn't – unfortunately – remembered putting his cigarette down at the sound of the telephone bell
and not going back into the room again, he would have
thought they'd set fire to the place themselves. They were
devils enough for anything . . . But the captain of the fire
brigade was shaking hands with them and obviously expecting him to do the same. He did it, muttering unintelligible

thanks and congratulations. William savoured the moment to the full, then said carelessly:

'I s'pose you won't be goin' round to see our fathers tonight?'

'N – n – n – no,' stammered Section Officer Perkins. 'No, of course not.' He was thoughtfully silent for a moment, then went on: 'Er – how did you come to see the fire at all? You couldn't have seen it from the road.'

But William hadn't thought out the answer to that question yet. He pretended not to hear it.

'Come on,' he said to his Outlaws. 'Time we went home to tea.'

CHAPTER 4

THE OUTLAWS AND THE PARACHUTIST

'GET out of here, you kids!' said the Home Guard man impatiently.

William and the Outlaws withdrew a few steps and continued to watch the fascinating spectacle – Home Guard men with tin hats and uniforms, carrying rifles and manning a fortress of camouflaged sandbags with loopholes for shooting through. It was incredibly impressive, exciting and romantic . . .

'I said, get on *out* of here,' repeated the Home Guard man, advancing threateningly upon them.

The Outlaws knew, of course, that he was only Billy Foxton, the blacksmith, who had let them watch him shoe horses and even occasionally lend a hand, but the tin hat, uniform and rifle invested him with such majesty that, obeying reluctantly, they turned and wandered disconsolately down the road.

'Gosh! I wish I was grown-up,' said William. 'They have all the fun.'

'An' I bet you anythin' the war'll be over by the time

we're grown up,' said Ginger. 'I bet you *anythin'* it will. I bet that when we're grown up we'll jus' have to go to offices with no fun at all. Grown-ups didn't have any fun till this war started, an' they won't have any more when it's over.'

'Fancy Billy Foxton with a uniform an' a gun an' a tin hat.'

'They've got wire things they can put right across the road, too.'

'I know . . . Tank traps,' said Henry.

'Crumbs! Wun't you like to shoot through one of those little holes?'

'One of 'em brought down a German plane the other day.'

'Our cook's cousin's a 'contamination man. He wears things jus' like a diver.'

'I'd sooner be a Home Guard man. I'd like to shoot through the little holes.'

'Our gardener knows a man what's got a friend what knows someone what caught a parachutist dressed up as a woman.'

'Gosh!'

'They do that, you know. They dress up as women.'

'Crumbs!'

'Yes, if ever you see a woman what looks like a man

you c'n be jolly sure it's a parachutist. If we were one of *them* we'd jus' put that wire thing across the road an' start shootin' at 'em through the little holes. Jus' think! They might find one any minute any day. Or whole armies of 'em. An' all we've gotter do,' in a tone of bitter disgust, 'is jus' do nothin'. It's not fair.'

'An' I bet we could do it all as well as them,' said Ginger.

'I jolly well bet we'd do it better.'

'An' I don't see why we shouldn't.'

'They wouldn't let us.'

'Don't see how they could stop us. We'd have one of our own. Somewhere where they've not got one. I bet there's lots of places where they've not got one. An' I bet if we did we'd catch a parachutist before they did.'

'It wasn't much good when we had an A.F.S.,' said Douglas.

'No, but we had it too near the other one,' explained William. 'They got jealous an' there was that mess-up about that fire . . . I say, we could get a thing to put across the road, an' we could make a fort with holes in.'

'They'd find out we'd got one an' stop us,' said Henry again.

'Bet they wouldn't,' said William, the optimist. 'We'd go somewhere where they couldn't see us. Gosh! There's *hundreds* of roads an' lanes an' places where they haven't got 'em, an' where those ole parachutists might easily come along . . . Well, I think it's our *juty* to have one.'

They considered this aspect of the question in silence. William was, as ever, persuasive, convincing his hearers even against their will.

'We've got no guns,' said Douglas at last.

'Well, we've got weapons, haven't we?' said William. '*Weapons* is all you need. We've got an air-gun haven't we, an' a pea-shooter, an' catapults, an' bows an' arrows, haven't we? Gosh! I nearly killed our gard'ner with a pea-shooter. At least he told my father I did, an' my father nearly killed me for it. An' I bet I can't count the windows an' things I've broke with my bow an' arrows an' catapult. If they'd all been Germans I bet the war'd 've been over by now.'

'We haven't got little holes to shoot through,' said Henry.

'We can make 'em, can't we?' said William. 'Anyone can make *holes,* can't they? Well, holes are *there* ready. You've only got to put somethin' round 'em.'

'Where'll we have it?' said Ginger.

'Somewhere where they can't see us,' said William. 'They'll only start bein' jealous an' try to stop us if they see us. They jus' won't *b'lieve* that we can do it as well as what they can. Grown-ups never do . . .' He paused a

moment and considered. 'There's that lane that goes from
Hadley Road to Marleigh. They've got nothin' there, an' I
bet the Germans could use it as a short cut to get to
Hadley. They've not thought of that – those ole Home
Guard men. They've put forts an' traps an' things all on
the main road an' forgot that that lane's a short cut.'

'It's too small for tanks to go along,' objected Henry.

'Yes, but parachutists dressed up as women could go
along it,' said William earnestly, 'an' I bet they *will*, too, if
we don't make a fort there. I bet we've gotter do it jolly
quick, too . . . They might be comin' tonight for all we
know.'

'There's those ole packing-cases in the ole barn,' said
Ginger thoughtfully. 'We could use them.'

'An' we've got some ole sandbags,' added Douglas.
'They took 'em away from in front of our shelter an' built
a sort of wall instead.'

'An' we've got lots an' lots of wooden seed boxes in our
shed,' said Henry. 'I bet we could fill 'em up with earth an'
they'd do as well as sandbags . . . I bet our gardener won't
notice they've gone.'

'An' there's some green paint in our garage,' said
Ginger. 'That'll do for camouflage.'

'*Gosh!*' breathed William ecstatically. 'We're going to
have a *jolly* fine one.'

The Outlaws and the Parachutist

*

It took the Outlaws all day to erect the 'fort' to their satisfaction. As it happened, no one passed by except a butcher's boy, who was so deeply interested in the proceedings that the butcher was receiving complaints all afternoon of joints delivered too late for lunch, and a village ancient, who was, apparently, so absorbed in memories of the past that he did not even notice it. By dusk it was completed. It was a somewhat fantastic erection, taking up, in fact, most of the roadway. At the base were the seed boxes from Henry's tool shed filled with earth and piled on top of each other. Above these came the sandbags laboriously carried from Douglas's air-raid shelter, and arranged so as to leave at intervals gaps forming the 'shooting holes', which were the crowning glory of the whole thing. Above this were ranged packing-cases brought from loft or boxroom as well as the old barn. The whole looked so crazy that you would have thought it would come down at a breath, but by some miracle of balance it resisted the force of gravity. Four large stones 'borrowed' from Ethel's rockery were placed at intervals across the remainder of the road to form a 'tank trap'. As William pointed out, there was no reason why a parachutist should not land with a small portable tank along with his motor bicycle and other equipment. Finally, the

Outlaws took up their positions in the rear of the fort pointing arrows, air-guns, pea-shooter and catapult through the 'shooting holes'.

The minutes passed. The lane remained deserted. Dusk began to fall.

'We've jus' not gotter mind nothin' happ'nin' at first,' William encouraged his band. '*They've* been waitin' for months an' months . . . We've jus' not gotter mind waitin' months an' months, but it *might* happen any minute. Any minute we might see a man dressed up like a woman comin' down the lane an' when you see a man dressed up like a woman you jolly well *know* he's a German parachutist. You—'

'Someone's comin' down now,' Ginger whispered excitedly. '*Gosh!* It looks someone queer, too. Bet you anythin' it's a parachutist.'

The figure approached. It was a large, unwieldy figure. It wore a curious feather-trimmed bonnet tied under its chin, a rusty black cape, and long, voluminous black skirts. The face beneath the bonnet showed masculine and heavy-featured through the dusk. Stout boots, suggesting of a farm labourer's, appeared beneath the rusty skirts.

'It *is* one of 'em,' whispered William tensely. 'It's – one, two, three – *fire!*'

'IT IS ONE OF 'EM,' WHISPERED WILLIAM TENSELY. 'IT'S –
ONE, TWO, THREE – *FIRE!*'

Air-gun, arrows, pea-shooter and catapult dis-
charged themselves from behind the 'fort' with such
devastating effect that the whole ramshackle structure
quivered and collapsed, hurling seed boxes, sandbags,
packing-cases and Outlaws in glorious confusion to the
ground. Having extricated themselves with some difficulty, they retrieved their weapons and looked round for
the parachutist. The parachutist lay outstretched and
motionless in the middle of the road. In falling beneath

the barrage of seed boxes, sandbags, packing-cases and human boys, he had hit his head against one of the rockery stones that formed the 'tank trap' and was apparently, for the time being at any rate, knocked out. It was certainly a case of 'he'. Bonnet and wig had rolled off, revealing a cropped head surmounting an unmistakable male countenance, and the large hands and boots removed all possible further doubt.

'Gosh!' breathed William. 'It *is* one!'

'Is he dead?' said Ginger apprehensively. 'We'll get in an awful row if he's dead.'

William approached the prostrate figure and examined it cautiously.

'No, it's all right,' he said. 'He's still breathing. He must've fainted or somethin'.'

'Hadn't we better go'n' fetch someone quick?' said Douglas nervously. 'He might come to, any minute, an' he looks jolly strong.'

'I wonder what's in his bag,' said William, picking up the old-fashioned reticule that lay in the road beside the parachutist.

He opened it and drew out a paper. The Outlaws crowded round.

'*Gosh!*' said William. 'It's a pass into Marleigh Aerodrome. *Gosh!* He's one of 'em, all right. He came over in a parachute dressed up as a woman with a forged pass into Marleigh Aerodrome.'

He examined the paper intently in the fading light. 'Yes, it's forged, all right,' he pronounced at last. 'It's jolly well forged, too. Gosh! We only jus' got him in time. He'd've blown up the whole place by now.'

They stood looking down uncertainly at their unconscious captive.

'What'll we do with him?' demanded Ginger.

'We've gotter get him to the police,' said William.

'How?' demanded Douglas. 'He'd be jolly heavy to carry an' he's goin' to be mad when he comes to. He'll prob'ly kill us all an' then go off to Marleigh Aerodrome an' blow it up, same as he'd meant to when we stopped him.'

'Tell you what we'll do,' said William. He turned to Douglas and Henry. 'You go an' fetch the police, an' Ginger and me'll guard him.'

'All right,' said Douglas, obviously relieved to be dismissed. 'All right. We'll be as quick as we can. Tell you what. We'll fetch Major Winton. His house is the nearest an' he's a Special Constable. Come on, Henry.'

Douglas and Henry vanished into the dusk.

William and Ginger stood guard over the prisoner. William held the bow and arrow, Ginger the air-gun. They looked down somewhat apprehensively at the motionless form. Though motionless, it was massive and muscular.

'I dunno that this bow 'n' arrow's goin' to be much good,' said William. 'He's too near to take aim prop'ly.'

'Same with the catapult,' said Ginger. 'He'd jump up and be on us before we'd took aim at him.'

'A stick's what we want,' said William reflectively. 'A good strong stick. Then, when he starts gettin' up we'll jus' hit him on the head with it, an' stun him again till the p'lice come.' He glanced across the field at the dim outline of the woods. 'It wouldn't take us a minute to go'n' get one. We'd be back before he's come unstunned.'

'All right,' agreed Ginger. 'Come on.'

They ran across the field into the wood and began to look round for a stout stick. It took longer than they had expected to find one.

'This'll do,' said William breathlessly at last, seizing upon a stout piece of ash about the size of a walking stick. 'Come on. Let's go back, quick . . . If he's started comin' unstunned an' the police aren't there yet, I'll give him a good hit with it . . .'

They hurried back to the road.

The fallen fortress was still there.

The 'tank trap' was still there.

But the captured parachutist had vanished . . .

They stared down incredulously at the spot where they had left him.

'Gosh!' said William at last faintly, and Ginger echoed '*Gosh!*'

'He's gone,' said William. 'He's come to an' gone. He's probably blown up Marleigh Aerodrome by now.'

'He's not got his forged pass,' Ginger reminded him. 'He can't get in without his forged pass.'

'He'll get in somehow,' said William. 'They're jolly clever, are parachutists. They train 'em special to be clever. He'll probably pretend to be a W.A.F.S.'s mother or somethin'.'

'Let's have a good look for him first,' said Ginger, 'case he's hidin' somewhere round. Keep the stick ready case he jumps out at us.'

But an exhaustive search of the lane with its bordering fields and hedges failed to produce any trace of the missing parachutist.

'I bet no one'll believe we found him,' said Ginger dejectedly.

'Course they will,' said William. 'We've got his forged pass, haven't we?'

'Well, I bet he's waitin' somewhere round to spring out on us an' get his pass back,' said Ginger. 'Tell you what. I think we oughter take his pass to the police station 'stead of hangin' about with it like this. It's all the proof we've got now he's gone.'

'All right,' said William. 'You take it along to the police station, an' I'll stay here till Douglas and Henry come. They oughter be here any minute.'

Ginger vanished into the dusk in the direction of the village and William continued a desultory search of the hedges.

Suddenly voices warned him of the approach of Douglas and Henry, and Major Winton. Major Winton, roused from a comfortable doze in his favourite armchair, had listened to their story, first with bewilderment then with incredulity. Finally, so convinced and convincing were the two Outlaws, he had begun to think that there might be something in it. After all, such things had happened in other countries and, impossible as it still seemed, might happen in this.

He stood in the roadway and looked about him – bewildered and still slightly fretful, as a man has a right to be who has been recently roused from a fireside doze. He was tall and thin, had long drooping moustaches and bore a striking resemblance to the White Knight in *Alice Through the Looking Glass*.

He stood in the road and looked about him.

'Well, where is he, where is he?' he said irritably, 'and what's all this frightful mess?'

'He's gone,' said William, 'and that's our fort.'

Major Winton looked at him suspiciously.

'If you boys have been playing a trick on me,' he began.

'Honest, we haven't,' William assured him. 'He was a parachutist dressed up as a woman and he'd got a forged pass into Marleigh Aerodrome.'

'Well, where is he?' said the major testily, 'and where's the pass?'

'We don't know about him,' said William. 'He got away. But we've got his pass all right. Ginger's jus' taken it to the p'lice station.'

At that moment a policeman appeared. He was a large, stout, official-looking policeman.

'Now then!' he said. 'What's all this 'ere?'

The major hailed his appearance with relief.

'These boys say they found a parachutist with a pass into Marleigh Aerodrome,' he said.

'Good!' said the policeman. 'He's the man we've been looking for, then. Someone's just rung up the station to say that he was attacked and his pass stolen from him.'

'Who attacked him?' asked Major Winton with interest.

'He doesn't know. He was knocked out at once, and when he recovered found that the pass was gone. Presumably it was the parachutist these kids say they found.' He turned to William. 'How d'you know he was a parachutist?'

'He was dressed like a woman,' explained William.

'Which way did he go?'

'I dunno,' said William. 'He ran away while we were getting a stick.'

'Where's the pass?'

'Ginger's got it. He's taking it to the police station.'

The policeman assumed an air of official dignity.

'*THAT'S* HIM!' CRIED WILLIAM
EXCITEDLY.

'I'll go and ask the Home Guard men if they've seen any suspicious-looking characters on the road,' he said. 'You kids stay here. We may want you again.'

And at that moment the parachutist suddenly arrived holding Ginger by the neck. He strode along, his rusty skirts billowing about his stout boots. His face looked set and stern. In his free hand he carried his bonnet and wig.

'*That's* him!' cried William excitedly. 'Catch him quick before he gets away.'

'CATCH HIM QUICK BEFORE HE GETS AWAY!'

'I've got the wretch,' the parachutist was saying to the policeman. 'It was this little villain who pinched my pass, though how he managed to knock me out beats me.'

The policeman blinked and stared and finally, forgetting his official dignity, murmured 'Blimey!'

Then to be on the safe side he put one hand on the parachutist's shoulder and the other on Ginger's.

129

'Here!' said the parachutist indignantly, as he shook it off. 'I've got to be at the aerodrome by seven-thirty. I've given this boy into custody and I can't waste any more time.'

'I like that,' burst out William indignantly. 'It's us givin' *you* into custody. *You're* the parachutist with a forged pass dressed up as a woman an' *we've* caught you.'

'The – *what*?' said the man.

'If you aren't a parachutist,' said William triumphantly, 'why are you dressed up as a woman with a forged pass?'

'Now then, now then, now then!' said the policeman, taking out his note-book. 'Let's get this straight . . .'

'I'm dressed up as a woman,' said the parachutist to William, 'because I'm going to give a performance at Marleigh Aerodrome and I have to be back at the Grand Theatre, Hadley, in time for the eight-thirty performance there, so I've no time to change afterwards. I'd no time to change before because I've been rehearsing at the Grand Theatre, Hadley, up to about half an hour ago. I thought I might risk driving there and back in costume but unfortunately my car broke down on the way, and I was taking a short cut down the lane to the garage on the main road to get help. And my pass is *not* forged. It was issued to me by the commanding officer of the camp in my capacity of guest artist at the variety show they're giving there this evening. They put my "turn" early so that I could get back in time for my "turn" at Hadley, but I'm going to be late I'm afraid. Anything else you'd like to know?'

'Then you aren't a German parachutist dressed up as a woman?' said William.

'Certainly not,' said the parachutist indignantly. 'Whatever made you think I was?'

'Corks!' said William, with a deep sigh. 'We never have any luck.'

'You an' your parachutists!' said the policeman shutting his note-book with a snap. 'An' a nice mess you've made of the road,' he added severely.

'That was our fort,' said Ginger mournfully.

'Well, I can't waste any more time here,' said Major Winton. 'Goodnight, sir,' to the parachutist.

'Goodnight, constable. And I hope that you boys won't make nuisances of yourselves like this again.'

He went home to finish his nap, feeling half relieved and half disappointed that the affair had petered out so tamely.

'I'll be goin', too,' said the policeman. 'Can't hang about here all night. Thank you, sir,' as the parachutist slipped something into his hand. 'Glad that it's all been settled satisfactorily. And, you kids,' to the Outlaws, 'be a bit more careful next time or you'll be getting into trouble.'

He went off, leaving parachutist and Outlaws alone.

'Well, we *thought* you were one,' said William in a small voice.

The parachutist looked down at the four dejected faces.

'I say,' he said suddenly, 'how would you like to come to the aerodrome with me and see the show?'

The four dejected faces beamed, sparkled, radiated.

'*Oh!*' gasped William. '*Could* we?'

'I think so,' said the parachutist. 'I think I can manage it. There's the question of your parents, of course . . . Suppose you come with me to the garage now and I'll ring them up from there and ask permission . . .'

The Outlaws sat in a crowded hall surrounded by a god-like company of men in Air Force blue – men who sailed the skies and brought down German bombers as regularly and unconcernedly as you and I have marmalade for breakfast.

That in itself would have provided one of the greatest thrills of the Outlaws' lives. But, added to this, the god-like beings were jovial and friendly. They teased Ginger about the colour of his hair. They called William Old Bill.

They gave them humbugs and pear drops.

The parachutist was beginning his repertoire of comic songs from the stage, a repertoire abounding in the immemorial jokes of the music hall.

As a comedian the parachutist had a way with him.

The audience rocked and roared helplessly.

The Outlaws rocked and roared with the best.

William choked till the tears ran down his face.

Ginger's yell of laughter at each fresh sally was like a gun explosion.

Douglas waved and stamped to swell the applause.

Henry was so purple in the face that, had anyone noticed him (which no one did), they would have diagnosed the last stages of an apoplectic fit.

It was the happiest day of their lives.

CHAPTER 5

WILLIAM – THE SALVAGE COLLECTOR

'COME on, William,' called Mrs Brown. 'The siren!' William stumbled sleepily out of bed, hunched into his dressing-gown, put on his bedroom slippers, collected various bits of cardboard that he was using for his 'invention' of an entirely new type of aeroplane, and made his way to the air-raid shelter at the bottom of the garden. Already assembled were Ethel, wearing a siren suit of pale grey corduroy, Emma the housemaid, in a red flannel dressing-gown, her hair in curling papers, her face grim and set, her teeth clasped firmly on an enormous cork, and Mr Brown, looking sleepy and dishevelled but preparing to re-read his evening paper, with an air of philosophical detachment.

Robert was on night duty at the warden's post, and Cook had joined the A.T.S. last week.

Ethel groaned as William entered.

'Oh gosh!' she said. 'I hoped he'd have slept through it.'

'Of course not,' said Mrs Brown placidly. 'I shouldn't dream of letting him sleep through it. Now, make room for him, dear, and don't be disagreeable.'

134

'Can't I have the hammock?' pleaded William.

Originally a hammock had been slung up for William's use, but the acrobatics in which he had indulged had precipitated him so frequently upon the heads of his family below that, much to his disgust, it had been taken down.

'No, dear,' said Mrs Brown. 'You only fidget and fall on people.'

'What can I do, then?' demanded William.

'Go to sleep,' said Mrs Brown. 'It's long past your bed-time.'

'*Sleep?*' echoed William in disgust. 'I jolly well wouldn't waste an air raid *sleepin*' in it.'

'Well, you must be quiet.'

'All right,' said William. 'I'll go on with my aeroplane. I bet it'll make 'em all sit up when I've finished it. It's a troop-carryin' aeroplane, an' it's goin' to go six hundred miles an hour an' it's goin' to be camouflaged so's to look like a cloud in the sky an' like a barn when it comes down so's the troops can hide in it.'

He stopped and listened for a few moments. 'That's a Dornier,' he pronounced with an air of finality.

'On the contrary, it's a cow,' said Mr Brown, without looking up from his paper.

'Oh, yes, so it is,' agreed William as he recognised the

note. 'It's Farmer Smith's Daisy. She's been carryin' on like that all day.'

Mrs Brown was checking her equipment of spirit kettle, biscuit tins, tea, coffee, milk, fruit and chocolate. She delighted in feeding her family during an air raid, but usually only William appreciated her efforts.

'Anyone like anything to eat or drink?' she asked hopefully.

'Yes, please,' said William promptly.

She gave him a glass of lemonade and a couple of biscuits.

'Wouldn't anyone else like something?' she asked. 'Tea or coffee or something?'

'Good heavens, Mother!' said Ethel, 'we can't go on eating all night.'

Mr Brown glanced at his watch.

'We've only just had dinner, my dear,' he said. 'The process of digestion can hardly be completed yet.'

Emma, appealed to next, shook her head grimly and pointed to her cork. Regretfully Mrs Brown put her equipment away.

Ethel had taken a small mirror from her bag and was patting her erection of red-gold curls.

'Thank heaven I had a perm last week,' she said. 'I simply couldn't have gone through another raid if I hadn't.'

'I don't quite see how you could have avoided it,' said Mr Brown, turning over a sheet of his evening paper.

'I do hope Robert's all right,' sighed Mrs Brown.

'Why shouldn't he be?' said Mr Brown. 'He couldn't very well have got anything more than a chill up to the present.'

'Yes, dear,' said Mrs Brown reproachfully, 'but, after all, it *is* a raid.'

Mr Brown gave an unfeeling grunt and turned over another sheet of his newspaper.

'Industrials seem to be keeping up pretty well,' he commented.

'*That's* a Dornier,' said William suddenly. 'Right over us, too,' he added in a tone of deep satisfaction.

'That is a motor cycle on the main road,' put in Mr Brown quietly, without looking up from his paper.

'Oh, yes . . . well, they do sound jolly alike.'

'Have you ever heard a Dornier?' asked his father.

'Well, I don't know. I may've done . . . This aeroplane's goin' to have six engines . . . Can I have somethin' else to eat, Mother? I'm jolly hungry.'

'There's the biscuit tin.'

'Can't I have some chocolate?'

'Not yet.'

'I think you might let me have a bit of chocolate. I

might be blown up any minute, an' you'd be jolly sorry afterwards that you'd not let me have a bit of chocolate.'

Mr Brown glanced up from his paper.

'Your nuisance value, William,' he said, 'is so inestimably high that I'm sure you're the last person in England Hitler would wish to bomb.'

'I bet it's me he's tryin' to get all the time,' said William. 'I bet he's heard about this aeroplane I'm makin'.'

'I'm going to go on knitting that blue jumper,' said Ethel. 'I still think it's the wrong blue, but the war's simply played havoc with shades.'

'Will there be enough of that cold lamb for tomorrow, Emma?' said Mrs Brown.

She and Emma were together supplying the place of Cook, and each treated the other with pitying contempt as an amateur.

'Oh yes, m'm. Lots,' said Emma through the cork.

'I'll make a pie for the sweet,' went on Mrs Brown, 'and we'll use up some of those pulped gooseberries.'

'No need for you to do that, m'm,' said Emma, removing the cork, her eyes gleaming with the light of battle. 'I'll have ample time to run up a suet pudden. The master always likes my suet puddens.'

'Very well, Emma,' said Mrs Brown, retreating, 'but those pulped gooseberries aren't keeping any too well.'

'One of them war-time recipes,' said Emma with a grimace expressing fastidious disgust. 'I've never trusted 'em. I warned both you an' Cook at the time, m'm, if you remember.'

With that she replaced her cork in a manner to preclude all further argument.

'Can I have the air-cushion, Mother?' said William.

'What for?'

'To – to rest on,' said William. 'My back aches.'

'Well, you know you broke the last one with playing with it. You can have it on condition you don't play with it.'

'All right, I don't want it, then,' said William.

'And what *have* you got in your dressing-gown pocket?' Mrs Brown leant forward and drew out a length of string, a penknife, a lump of putty, a handful of marbles, some screws, a match-box containing a live beetle, and a tube of glue, most of whose contents had already escaped.

'Don't let the beetle out,' said William anxiously. 'It's one of the best I've ever had. I'm jus' goin' to give it a bit of biscuit.'

'If anyone lets it out, I'll *die*,' threatened Ethel.

'The glue's simply *soaked* through your dressing-gown,' said Mrs Brown . . . 'Oh well,' resignedly, 'I can't do anything about it now . . . Do stop eating biscuits, William. You've had quite enough.'

'I bet that was a screaming bomb,' said William.

'It was the twelve-thirty letting off steam,' said Mr Brown.

'Was it?' said William despondently. 'It's been a rotten raid so far.'

'I wonder if the Bevertons are coming,' said Ethel.

'The *who*?' said Mr Brown, looking up from his paper.

Ethel and Mrs Brown exchanged nervous glances.

'Yes, didn't we tell you, dear?' said Mrs Brown. 'The Bevertons asked if they could share our shelter and we didn't like to say "no".'

'Good heavens! They've got one of their own.'

'I know, but they say it's so much jollier to be together. They were sharing the Mertons' last week, but Bella quarrelled with Dorita so they asked if they could share ours.'

'Bella?' demanded Mr Brown.

'Bella Beverton, dear,' explained his wife. 'One of Ethel's friends. Don't you remember her?'

'Ethel's friends are indistinguishable,' said Mr Brown. 'Their vocabulary is limited to the word "marvellous", but they can say it in twenty different tones of voice. Why intensify the horrors of war by having them in the air-raid shelter?'

'Perhaps they won't come, dear,' said Mrs Brown soothingly. 'After all, it's some time since the siren went.'

'They always take a long time getting ready,' said Ethel.

'Ready? What for?' said Mr Brown.

'For air-raid shelters,' said Ethel.

'Gosh,' said William excitedly. 'I can hear bombs.'

But it was only the Bevertons arriving.

Mrs Beverton was inordinately stout and her daughter was inordinately thin. They were both dressed in the latest in siren suits, and had obviously taken great pains with

'GOSH!' SAID WILLIAM EXCITEDLY. 'I CAN HEAR BOMBS.' BUT IT WAS ONLY THE BEVERTONS ARRIVING.

their make-up and *coiffeurs*. Mrs Beverton wore a three-stringed pearl necklace, large jade earrings and four bracelets. She had, moreover, used a new exotic perfume that made William cry out in genuine alarm, 'Gas! Where's my gas mask?'

'So sorry we're late,' she said gaily as she entered. 'We just had to finish off our new siren suits. We've been working on them all day but they just needed the finishing touches, as it were. I had to get out my jewellery, too. I always like to feel I've got it with me, as it were. Room for a little one?'

She plunged down on to a small camp mattress next to Mr Brown, almost blocking him from view.

'Not squashing you, I hope?' she inquired politely.

'Not at all,' came the muffled voice of Mr Brown from between her and the wall of the shelter.

Bella sat down by Ethel and took out her knitting.

'I'm making a green jumper like that one of yours,' she said. 'Did you get your perm?'

'Yes. Yesterday.'

'I shall have to have another soon if the raids keep on.'

'Now you'd all like something to eat and drink, wouldn't you?' said Mrs Brown happily, setting to work on her tea equipage and adding almost mechanically. 'I do hope Robert's all right.'

'SO SORRY WE'RE LATE,' SAID MRS BEVERTON GAILY AS SHE
ENTERED.

'Do you like this colour?' said Ethel, holding up the
jumper she was working on.

'Marvellous!' said Bella in a deep voice.

'I want to get it finished by tomorrow. I like the yoke
effect, don't you?'

'Marvellous!' said Bella on a higher key.

'Did you see the cardigan Dolly Clavis knitted, with a
hood? She's going to lend me the pattern. It'll be useful for
cold mornings.'

'*Marvellous!*' squeaked Bella ecstatically.

'You'll have a cup of tea, won't you, dear?' said Mrs Brown to her husband.

But Mr Brown wasn't there. At Bella's third '*Marvellous!*' he had crept quietly out of the emergency exit.

'Isn't he *tiresome*!' sighed Mrs Brown. 'Now, William, you can have one more biscuit and then you must lie down and try to sleep.'

'Sleep!' echoed William indignantly, but his eyelids were heavy and it was all he could do to keep them open.

Mrs Beverton had embarked upon a sea of prattle.

'This scrap-iron business is simply disgraceful,' she said. 'It's the same everywhere. They made a terrific effort just at the beginning and then let things slide. There must be lots more scrap iron about by now, that no one's troubled to collect.'

William gradually surrendered to the tide of sleep that was engulfing him. Through it he heard an occasional 'Marvellous!' from Bella, or a 'I do hope that Robert and your father are all right,' from his mother.

He slept through the All Clear but was roused by Mrs Brown. He gathered his scattered pieces of aeroplane sleepily together.

Mrs Beverton was still in full sail on her sea of prattle. 'This cousin of mine,' she was saying, 'made quite a little sum for the Spitfire Fund by this exhibition – just bits of shrapnel and a piece of a Dornier, and part of a shell-casing and a German incendiary bomb and a few things like that. People paid a shilling admission and she's promised to lend it to me and—'

Mrs Brown smothered a yawn.

'That was the "All Clear",' she said. 'Shall we go back to bed?'

'What a shame!' said Mrs Beverton. 'I always hate leaving a party.'

Ethel sat up and rubbed her eyes.

'We had quite a nice little nap,' she said to Bella, 'didn't we?'

'Marvellous,' yawned Bella.

As William, back in his own bed, yielded once more to sleep, his thoughts went over what Mrs Beverton had been saying just before he went to sleep in the shelter. No one was collecting scrap iron . . . people ought to be collecting scrap iron . . . people ought to be . . . people ought to . . . people ought . . . He fell asleep and dreamed that Hitler, wearing Mrs Beverton's siren suit, and Emma (still with the cork in her mouth) were wheeling a handcart of scrap iron, which turned into a gigantic aeroplane in the shape of a beetle which turned into Farmer Smith's Daisy.

He awoke with the firm conviction that he must do something about scrap iron.

Most of his previous war efforts had been unsuccessful but, he decided, they had, perhaps, been too ambitious. He had tried to capture spies and parachutists, and this had turned out to be more difficult than he had thought it would. He couldn't go wrong collecting scrap iron. Nobody could go wrong collecting scrap iron . . . You just – well you just collected scrap iron, and then took it to the depot in Hadley.

He remembered that the organisers of the original appeal for scrap iron had had notices printed and dropped through letter-boxes, asking people to collect their scrap iron and advising them that it would be called for on a certain day. That, then, obviously, was the way to set about it . . .

He assembled his Outlaws that morning and expounded his scheme to them.

'We'll write notices,' he said, 'and put them into people's letter-boxes, an' then, when they've had time to get the scrap iron together, we'll go round an' collect it. We can use my wooden cart or a wheelbarrow or some-thin'. An' I bet they'll be jolly grateful to us.'

The composition of his 'appeal' took some time, as none of them could remember exactly how the original one had been worded. The final effort was chiefly William's.

SKRAPPION

Pleese collect your skrappion and we will call for it
tomorro.

By order, William Brown.

They spent several hours copying it out and took it
round the village in the evening.

There was another air-raid alarm that night, and again
Mrs Beverton and Bella joined the Browns in their shelter.
Again Mrs Beverton prattled merrily all night. This time she
knitted as well, taking up, as it seemed, almost the entire
shelter with elbow acrobatics and running a knitting needle
into Mr Brown's eye three or four times before he finally
took to flight. Again Bella said 'Marvellous!' fifty times in
fifty different tones of voice. Again Emma wore her cork,
taking it out only to snub Mrs Brown when she suggested
making a milk pudding for lunch the next day. Again the
only recognisable sounds outside the shelter were the distant
lowing of Daisy and an occasional motorist.

William busied himself with his aeroplane and his
plans for collecting scrap iron. He was vaguely aware that
Mrs Beverton was prattling about a Spitfire Fund exhibition, and asking his mother to tea the next day, but was
too much occupied with his own affairs to listen to her.

The next afternoon the Outlaws set off to collect the

scrap iron. The result was at first disappointing. People were either amused or annoyed but in neither case did they produce any scrap iron. Mrs Monks they found specially irritating.

'No, children,' she said firmly, 'we can't be bothered to play games with you now. We have work to do for the country even if you haven't,' and vanished before they could explain that they had come on a matter of urgent national importance.

By the time they reached Miss Milton's they were definitely discouraged. Miss Milton was discouraging at the best of times, and in view of their treatment by normally quite pleasant people they felt that it would be worse than useless to present themselves at the front door and demand scrap iron. They were, however, reluctant to leave the house without making some effort towards the attainment of their object.

'Let's go round to the back,' suggested William, 'I believe I remember seein' a lot of rubbish behind her tool shed. Her gardener found 'em in that bit of waste ground he was clearin' for the potatoes.'

They went round to the back and peeped over the hedge. Yes, there was the little heap of scrap iron that William remembered having seen – battered saucepans, rusty tin cans, old kettles . . .

'Crumbs!' said William. 'That's just what we want. An' *she* can't want it.' He glanced at the house. 'We won't bother her goin' to ask her. We'll jus' take it through the hedge. I bet that's the best thing to do. I bet she'd rather we did that than come to the house an' bother her . . . I'll get through and hand it out to you.'

He scrambled through the hedge and handed the pieces of scrap iron one by one to the others. They almost – not quite – filled the handcart.

'That's jolly good,' said William as they set off again. 'I bet she'll be jolly grateful to us when she finds out. Let's try Mrs Beverton next,' he suggested. 'She comes to our air-raid shelter, an' my father says she's worse than the air raid, but I bet she'll have a bit of scrap iron. I put one of the notices through her letter-box, anyway.'

They trundled the cart along to Mrs Beverton's house, opened her small front gate and wheeled it up the path towards the front door. And then William suddenly stopped. For the French windows of the morning-room were open and inside the morning-room, on a long trestle table, was what could be nothing other than a collection of scrap iron kindly left there for them by Mrs Beverton.

'*Corks!*' gasped William. 'That's *jolly* decent of her. She's jus' left 'em there ready for us so's we could get 'em

'*CORKS!*' GASPED WILLIAM. 'IT'S *JOLLY* DECENT OF HER.'
THE COLLECTION OF SCRAP IRON WAS CERTAINLY
IMPRESSIVE.

without botherin' her. It's *jolly* decent of her.'

He wheeled the cart across the lawn, put it down
beside the French window, and entered the morning room.

The collection of scrap iron was certainly impressive –
heavy pieces of metal, jagged pieces of metal, dull pieces
of metal of all textures, shapes and sizes.

'There's not room for it all in the cart,' said Ginger.

'No, but it's a jolly sight better than that stuff of ole Miss Milton's,' said William. 'It's jolly good scrap iron, an' it's jolly decent of her to put it out ready for us like this. I'd like to take it to Hadley first, before Miss Milton's. They'll be jolly pleased with it down at Hadley. I bet it'll be the best they ever had . . . I say! We could leave Miss Milton's ole stuff here, an' take this down to Hadley an' then come back for Miss Milton's, couldn't we? I bet that's a jolly good idea . . . Come on, let's take Miss Milton's out an' put this in. This'll just fill the cart nicely, an' then we can get a bit more to put with ole Miss Milton's an' make up the second cartful. Come on . . .'

In a few minutes they had emptied the cart, put its contents on the trestle table, and put the contents of the trestle table into the cart.

Then, with the pleased feeling of a patriotic duty satisfactorily accomplished, they set off to Hadley.

Mrs Beverton's preparations for the Spitfire Exhibition tea party were somewhat behindhand. She had taken her afternoon nap, as usual, and overslept, so that she was still harassing her little maid over the arrangements for tea when the guests were due to arrive.

Moreover, Bella, who was supposed to have copied out

the labels for the exhibits, so kindly lent by Mrs Beverton's cousin, had forgotten all about it, and was now hastily scribbling them upstairs in her bedroom. Bella was feeling rather disgruntled, firstly because she had not heard from her latest boy friend for over a week and secondly because she was beginning to have a horrible suspicion that the green jumper didn't suit her. So, though everything was still 'Marvellous', it was marvellous in a minor key.

'Bella, *do* hurry up with those labels,' called Mrs Beverton from downstairs. 'I thought you'd have got them done this morning.'

'I was busy,' said Bella petulantly. 'I was finishing that wretched jumper. I think it's a frightful colour.'

'Well, you would have it,' said Mrs Beverton unsympathetically.

'I know. It looked all right on Ethel.'

'Oh, well, any colour suits Ethel,' said Mrs Beverton. 'She's so pretty.'

'Marvellous,' said Bella tartly.

'Now do hurry up with those labels, dear. I can't think why you've been so long.'

Bella muttered something under her breath that certainly wasn't 'Marvellous', and scrawled the remaining half-dozen labels.

'I've finished them now, Mother.'

'Well, I wish you'd go and put them on the exhibits in the morning-room, dear. It's after four, and I've still got to change.'

'But I don't know which to put on which,' objected Bella.

'You can't go wrong, dear. I've put them in a straight line in order all along the table and the labels are numbered. Just put label number one on the one nearest the door and so on to the window. You can't go wrong, and I'm sure it's nice for you to feel that you're helping mother.'

'Marvellous!' said Bella in what she imagined to be a tone of cutting irony.

She took the labels down to the morning-room. She was still feeling aggrieved by her mother's reference to Ethel Brown. She never had been able to understand what people saw in Ethel Brown. Personally she thought that Ethel looked a perfect sight in the green jumper. She never had liked her hair. Or her voice. Or her eyes . . .

She stood in the doorway of the morning-room and looked with dispassionate contempt at the collection of metal on the table . . . It was the first time she had seen it (she had been out when it arrived) and it was, she thought, a pretty rotten show. It wasn't in a straight line either, whatever her mother might say. She straightened it and began to

153

put the labels round. 'Part of wing of Messerschmitt' (looked more like a rusty old saucepan). 'Piece of shell casing' (looked more like an old kettle lid – what you could see of it for rust). 'Part of aileron from Dornier 17' (more like an old sardine tin). She flung the labels down, anyhow, one by one. There were too many labels for the exhibits, but she didn't care. She wasn't interested in the rotten old exhibition, and she didn't care whether it was a success or not. After all, one would expect one's own mother to appreciate one's good points if no one else did. She had always thought that her hair, especially after a brightening shampoo, was a better colour than Ethel Brown's any day . . .

Mrs Beverton had changed into her mauve georgette just in time to breathlessly receive the first guest. There were so few social activities of any kind nowadays that all the invitations she sent out had been accepted even at such short notice. Mrs Monks was coming and Miss Milton and Mrs Bott and Mrs Clavis and Mrs Barton and Mrs Brown and Miss Blake and Miss Featherstone.

Mrs Beverton hurried breathlessly down to the drawing-room just as the little maid was admitting Mrs Barton. One by one but almost immediately afterwards (for the meaningless urban convention of arriving everywhere half an hour late was rightly held in scorn here) the others arrived.

'Do come in,' said Mrs Beverton brightly as she ushered them into the drawing-room. 'So nice of you to come to my little party. All in a good cause, isn't it? I thought that we'd have tea first and that while we were having it you could go one by one and see the exhibition. There really isn't room in the morning-room for all of us. I've put a plate on the table near the door, and if you'll all put your sixpence in that – or however much more you like to make it, of course . . . All the exhibits are numbered and described. Will you go first, Miss Featherstone? You know where the morning-room is, don't you? Just across the way . . .'

Miss Featherstone went out, and the others sat down and began tea. In a short time Miss Featherstone returned. She looked pale and bewildered.

'Well,' said Mrs Beverton with a complacent and expectant smile, 'did you find it interesting?'

'Er – yes,' said Miss Featherstone uncomfortably, avoiding her hostess's eye. 'Er – y-yes.'

'Tragic, of course, I agree,' said Mrs Beverton. 'Definitely tragic, of course. I quite understand how you feel. I'm not one to gloat over it myself. However you look at it, it means tragedy in one form or another . . . Now, Miss Blake, would you like to see it? Just pop your sixpence on to the plate. Or a bit more, of course, if you really like the show . . . You know the way to the morning-room, don't you? . . . A little more tea, Mrs Brown?'

A few moments later Miss Blake returned to the room. She, too, looked pale and bewildered.

'Well?' said Mrs Beverton again expectantly. 'It's interesting, isn't it?'

Miss Blake avoided both her hostess's eye and Miss Featherstone's as she stammered 'Er – yes,' and returned to her seat.

Mrs Beverton looked from her to Miss Featherstone in surprise. How odd people were nowadays! No interest in anything – not even a Spitfire Fund Exhibition. It must be the war, of course, and lack of sleep . . . She was glad it hadn't taken her like that.

One by one the other guests went in to see the exhibition, and all returned with that same air of bewilderment; that constrained and embarrassed manner.

'What do you think of it?' murmured Mrs Clavis to Mrs Barton under cover of the general conversation. 'Do you think that the war's turning her queer?'

'Well, the whole thing's most extraordinary,' said Mrs Barton. 'I can only put it down to lack of sleep. I hardly like to think it's a deliberate trick.'

'I'm not so sure,' said Mrs Clavis darkly. 'I'm really not so sure.'

'Odd that no one's *said* anything.'

'Well, one doesn't like to. I didn't give any money, did you?'

'Indeed, I did not,' said Mrs Barton. 'The thing's a deliberate fraud. At least it's a fraud, whether deliberate or not, it's not for me to decide.'

'I should think that Mrs Monks would *say* something,' said Miss Blake hopefully. 'I mean, it's supposed to be the duty of the church to speak *out*.'

Mrs Monks was at that moment entering the room, and it was quite clear that she was going to 'speak out'. She stood just inside the drawing-room door, fixing her eyes on Mrs Beverton in dramatic denunciation.

'Mrs Beverton,' she said in the voice that she generally kept for unruly choir boys. 'Mrs Beverton, I cannot allow you to continue this gross deception.'

Mrs Beverton gaped at her.

'Th-t-t-t-this what?' she said.

'This gross deception,' repeated Mrs Monks. 'This obtaining of money under false pretences for *whatever* purpose.'

'I – I don't understand you,' stammered Mrs Beverton. 'Really, Mrs Monks, I know that we're *all* suffering from lack of sleep, but—'

'Your exhibition is nothing but a collection of scrap iron of a particularly valueless description.'

'How *dare* you?' said Mrs Beverton. 'This collection was lent me by my cousin. She made two pounds, six shillings and tenpence halfpenny by it for her local Spitfire Fund, and you have the impertinence to say—'

Miss Milton now appeared in the doorway. She, too, had been in to see the 'Exhibition'. Her small precise figure quivered with indignation.

'This is an outrage, Mrs Beverton,' she said.

Mrs Beverton gazed helplessly from one to the other. *Two* of them suffering from delusions as a result of lack of sleep . . . 'What on *earth* do you mean, Miss Milton?' she said. 'I know that we've had to spend most of the nights in our shelter lately, and I know that— '

'You must be aware,' said Miss Milton, 'that your so-called exhibition is merely a collection of scrap iron purloined by means I do not understand from the back of my tool shed?'

'You're mad,' said Mrs Beverton. 'You *must* be mad.'

'I recognise every single piece,' said Miss Milton grimly. 'There's the old fish slice that I threw away because it was too small, and that you have the impertinence to label as part of a Dornier wing. There's that old saucepan that leaks and I had soldered twice, and that you've labelled as a German incendiary bomb. The whole thing is beneath contempt and an insult to our intelligence. It—'

Dazedly Mrs Beverton appealed to the others, but to her amazement they supported her accusers. They hadn't liked to *say* anything, but – well, Miss Milton and Mrs Monks were quite right. It was just a collection of scrap iron. They didn't know how Mrs Beverton had the face to play such a trick on them.

'This is a conspiracy,' said Mrs Beverton dramatically. 'Nothing other than a conspiracy.'

She swept into the morning-room, followed by her bewildered guests. At the door she stopped and stared at the line of rusty battered metal on the table.

'It's a German plot,' she gasped. 'It's the work of someone who wants to stop the money going to the Spitfire Fund.' Her eyes roved accusingly over her guests. 'One of you must be responsible. It was a genuine exhibition before you came, wasn't it, Bella?'

'Oh no, Mother,' said Bella calmly, 'it wasn't. It was just like this.'

'*What?*' said Mrs Beverton, clutching her head with both hands. 'Am I mad or are you?'

'Well, I'm not,' said Bella calmly.

At this point the little maid entered.

'It's that there William Brown, 'm,' she said. 'He says, thank you very much for the scrap iron an' he's come back for the lot he left here.'

'Oh dear, oh dear, oh dear!' groaned Mrs Brown. 'I had a *feeling* all along that William was at the bottom of it.'

'How simply marvellous!' squeaked Bella.

Mr Brown assumed his sternest expression when Mrs Brown laid the story before him that evening.

'I quite agree with you, my dear,' he said. 'The boy's getting hopelessly out of hand. Just because there's a war on he thinks he can be allowed to go about making a nuisance of himself to everyone. He needs a lesson, and I'll see that he gets it.'

'It was dreadful,' moaned Mrs Brown, 'and then when Mrs Beverton said in front of everyone that she wouldn't dream of using our air-raid shelter any more, I felt—'

'Said *what*?' demanded Mr Brown.

'That she wouldn't dream of using our air-raid shelter any more.'

'She – actually – said – that?' asked Mr Brown slowly.

'Yes. In fact she made arrangements then and there to join the Bartons.'

The look of severity faded from Mr Brown's face. As far as a face of his particular cast of grimness could be said to shine, it shone.

'So – she won't be coming if there's a raid tonight?'

'No, dear. But about William—'

'Yes, yes,' said Mr Brown impatiently. 'The boy obviously meant no harm. I can't see what you're making all this fuss about. Actually, when you come to think of it, he was trying to help. I can't understand why you're so hard on the child.'

'But—' began Mrs Brown.

'You're quite *sure* that the Bevertons aren't coming again?'

'Quite, dear.'

An almost seraphic smile spread over Mr Brown's countenance.

'How marvellous!' he quoted.

CHAPTER 6

WILLIAM AND THE BOMB

IT caused quite a sensation among the Outlaws when they heard that the Parfitts were coming back from London to live in the village again because of the war. Joan Parfitt was the only girl of whom the Outlaws had ever really approved. She was small and dark and shy and eager and considered the Outlaws the embodiments of every manly virtue. They were afraid that her sojourn in London might have spoilt her, but to their relief they found that she had not altered at all. She was still small and dark and shy and eager, and she still considered the Outlaws the embodiments of every manly virtue. She was not even infected by the bomb snobbery that the inhabitants of the village found so exasperating in most of its London visitors. She did not describe her methods of dealing with 'incendiaries', her reactions to 'screamers', her shelter life, the acrobatics she performed when taking cover at various sinister sounds.

The village was sick of such descriptions from evacuees. It was perhaps unduly sensitive on the subject, suffering

162

from what might be called a bomb inferiority complex. For, though enemy aeroplanes frequently roared overhead during the night watches, and a neighbouring A.A. gun occasionally made answer, providing the youthful population with the shrapnel necessary for their 'collections', no bombs had as yet fallen on the village.

Mrs Parfitt had taken Lilac Cottage, recently vacated by Miss Cliff, and there the Outlaws went to call for Joan the morning after her arrival.

'It's lovely to be back,' she greeted them. 'I can hardly believe it's true.'

The Outlaws were flattered by this attitude.

'I expect London's a bit more excitin' really,' said William modestly.

'London's *horrible*,' said Joan with a shudder. 'All streets and houses. I can't *tell* you how horrible it is.'

'Well, come on,' said William happily. 'Let's go to the woods an' play Red Indians.'

For in the old days Joan had always been their squaw, and no one else had ever been found to fill the role satisfactorily.

In the course of the morning, during which Joan showed no falling off in her squaw performance, it turned out that she would celebrate her birthday while she was staying in the village.

'And Mummy says I can have a birthday party,' she said. 'It would have been terribly dull in London, but it will be lovely to be able to have you all to a birthday party.'

Further investigation revealed that Joan's birthday was on the same day as Hubert Lane's. And then the Outlaws became really excited. For Hubert Lane – the inveterate enemy of the Outlaws – was having a birthday of (as far as possible) pre-war magnificence and he was inviting to it all his own supporters. He had, indeed, arranged the party chiefly in order to exclude from it the Outlaws and their friends and to jeer at them as the Boys who were not Going to a Birthday Party. He was aghast when he heard about Joan's. He continued to jeer, but a note of anxiety crept into his jeering.

'We're goin' to have jellies,' he shouted to the Outlaws, when he met them in the village.

'So're we,' the Outlaws shouted back.

'We're goin' to have a trifle.'

'So're we.'

'We're goin' to have crackers.'

'So're we.'

Joan's mother appreciated the importance of the occasion. Without aspiring to put Hubert's in the shade, the Outlaws' party (for so they looked on it) was to be every bit as good.

'We're goin' to get Mr Leicester to come an' bring his kinematograph,' said Hubert.

'He won't,' said William. 'He's a warden an' he says he's not got time. We've tried him.'

'Then we'll borrow it off him. My mother can work it.'

'So can Joan's mother, but he won't lend it. We've tried.'

'Huh!' said Hubert. 'I bet he'll lend it *us*.'

But he was wrong. Mr Leicester most emphatically refused either to bring his kinematograph to the party or to lend it.

In pre-war days the crowning glory of every children's party for miles round had been Mr Leicester's kinematograph. It was his greatest pride and joy, and he loved to take it about with him and show it off. No children's party indeed was complete without Mr Leicester, his kinematograph and his collection of Mickey Mouse films. No date was ever fixed for a party without first making sure that Mr Leicester would be free . . .

Since the war, however, Mr Leicester had become a District Warden and was taking life very seriously. He had no time for such childish things as kinematographs and had, in fact, locked it up in the big cupboard in his dressing-room, announcing that it would not reappear till after the war. He refused indignantly all suggestions that he should lend it. No one but he, he said, understood its delicate mechanism.

Approached by the organisers of both parties, Mr Leicester remained firm. Did they realise, he asked sternly, that there was a war on and that such things as kinematographs were wholly out of place? He would neither bring it nor lend it. It should not, in fact, see the light of day till Victory should have crowned the wardens' efforts (for Mr Leicester considered the war to be waged entirely by wardens, magnificently ignoring army, navy and air force). Then, and not till then, he would take it out, and it would accompany him on the usual round of local festivities . . .

Both the Outlaws and the Hubert Laneites finally resigned themselves to the absence of this central attraction, but rivalry between them still ran high.

'We're goin' to have some jolly excitin' games.'

'We're goin' to have some you've never heard of.'

'An' we're goin' to have some *you've* never heard of.'

'Anyway, you're not goin' to have Mr Leicester's cinema thing.'

'Neither are *you.*'

Hubert was afraid that the Outlaws, being admittedly more enterprising than his own followers, would evolve a more exciting programme for Joan's party than he and his followers could evolve for theirs.

'Wish somethin'd *happen* to them,' he muttered darkly as he passed Lilac Cottage and saw through the window Joan and her mother making decorations for the party out of some coloured paper left over from Christmas.

And – as if his wishes had the power of a magician's wand – something *did* happen.

The bomb fell that night.

It was literally a bomb.

For the first time since the outbreak of war a German bomber, passing over the village, chose, for no conceivable reason, to release part of its load there.

Fortunately, most of it fell in open country and there were no casualties, but one bomb fell in the roadway just outside the Hall, blew up the entrance gates and made a deep crater in the road.

Mr Leicester, complete with overalls and tin hat, was on the spot immediately. It was he who descried, at the bottom of the crater, the smooth rounded surface of a half-buried 'unexploded bomb'.

All through the months of inactivity he had longed for an Occasion to which he could rise, and he rose to this one superbly. The road must be roped off. Traffic must be diverted. All houses in the immediate neighbourhood must be evacuated. Fortunately the Botts were away, so the many complications that Mrs Bott would inevitably have introduced into the situation were absent. But Lilac Cottage was among the houses that Mr Leicester ordered to be evacuated, and at first Mrs Parfitt did not know where to go. Then Miss Milton came to the rescue. Miss Milton was prim and elderly and very very house-proud. She had had several evacuees billeted on her, but none of them had been able to stay the course and all had departed after a few weeks. So now she had a spare bedroom to offer Mrs Parfitt and Joan.

'I shall look on it as my war work,' she said to Mrs Parfitt. 'It will mean a good deal of inconvenience for me – I quite realise that – but one must put up with inconvenience these days.'

Mrs Parfitt hesitated.

'It's *very* kind of you,' she said at last. 'I hope, of course, that it won't be for long. Poor Joan! We were going to have her birthday party at the end of the month.'

Miss Milton paled.

'A *party*!' she gasped. 'She must not, of course, expect anything of that sort in *my* house. I was going to make it a condition that no other child entered the house at all. I have a *horror* of children, and I shall expect Joan to conform to the rules I laid down for my other evacuees . . . You will be coming at once, I suppose?'

Mrs Parfitt sighed.

'Yes . . . Thank you so much. I hope we shan't trouble you for long.'

But days passed and still the bomb failed to explode. The spirits of the Hubert Laneites rose.

'*Yah!*' they jeered. 'Who's not goin' to have a birthday party?'

They taunted Joan and the Outlaws with the dainties they were preparing for their own feast, following them through the village and shouting:

'Trifle . . . jellies . . . choc'late cake . . . An' *who's* not goin' to have any of 'em? *Yah!* Who's not goin' to have a party at all? *Yah!*'

It seemed, indeed, very unlikely that Joan's party would take place now. Mr Leicester would go at frequent intervals to lean over the barrier and gaze with fond but modest pride at his unexploded bomb.

'No,' he would say, 'I don't know when it will go off. It might go off any minute or it might not go off for weeks. I am taking every precaution.'

Meantime Joan was not finding life easy at Miss Milton's. Miss Milton had drawn up an elaborate code of rules. Joan was not to use the front door. She was to take off outdoor shoes immediately on entering the house. She was not to speak at meals. If inadvertently she touched any article of furniture, Miss Milton would leap at it with a duster, lips tightly compressed, in order to rub off any possible finger marks. Miss Milton rested upstairs in her bedroom from lunch time till tea time. She was, she said, a 'light sleeper', so Joan had to creep about the house during that time on tiptoe and not raise her voice above a whisper.

After a week of this both Joan and her mother began to look pale and worn, but it was not till the afternoon before the date of what was to have been her birthday party that Joan finally gave up hope. William found her sobbing at the bottom of Miss Milton's garden.

'I've been trying not to cry so as not to worry Mummy,' she sobbed, 'but I can't help it. Oh, William, it's horrible. I was looking forward to the party so much and it would have been tomorrow and I can't bear it . . . It's so hateful here and Miss Milton's always cross and Hubert Lane shouts out after me about the party whenever I go out and . . . Oh, I'm so miserable I don't know what to do.'

William considered the situation. He, too, had been pursued down the road from a safe distance by the jeers of the Hubert Laneites. Things seemed pretty hopeless . . .

'And they'll be worse still afterwards,' said Joan. 'They'll never let us forget it. I did so want to have the party tomorrow. Oh, William,' she fixed brimming eyes on him beseechingly, 'can't you *do* something about it?'

The appeal went to William's head. He could not meet

those tear-filled eyes and admit that he was powerless to help. He was not in any case a boy who liked to own himself at a loss . . .

He assumed an expression of dare-devil recklessness and set his cap at a gangster-like angle.

'You leave it to me,' he said between his teeth. 'I'll fix it . . .'

'YOU LEAVE IT TO ME,' SAID WILLIAM BETWEEN HIS TEETH.
'I'LL FIX IT . . .'

The tear-filled eyes widened. Hope shone through despair.

'Oh, William, *can* you?'

He gave a short laugh.

'Can I?' he repeated. 'Huh! *Can* I? There's not many things I can't do, let me tell you!'

'Oh, *William*, but . . .' Her face clouded again. 'Tomorrow? . . . It's so near.'

'Huh!' he snorted contemptuously. 'Tomorrow's nothin' to me, tomorrow isn't.'

Her small expressive face shone once more with hope and admiration.

'Oh William, you are wonderful!'

''Course I'll fix it up by tomorrow,' he said. 'Now jus' don't you worry about it any more. You jus' leave it all to me. I'll get it all fixed up for you by tomorrow easy. You'll have your party an' – an' ' – he lost his head still further – 'Mr Leicester'll bring his cinema thing an' it'll all be all right.'

One – comparatively sane – part of him seemed to raise its voice in protest as it heard these more than rash promises, but William turned a deaf ear to it.

'Everythin'll be all right,' he went on loudly as if to shout down the unseen opponent. 'You jus' leave it all to me.'

'An' we can go home tomorrow?' said Joan.

''Course you can,' said William.

Joan drew a deep sigh, smiling blissfully through her tears.

'Oh William!' she said. 'You are wonderful. *Thank* you!'

'Quite all right,' said William airily, though there was something fixed and glassy in the smile that answered hers. 'Well, I'd better be gettin' off to see about it.'

He swaggered out of the garden gate and set off down the road. As soon as he reached the bend that hid him from Joan's sight his swagger dropped from him and he began to argue fiercely as if with the still small voice of sanity . . . 'Well, why shouldn't I? . . . Well, I bet I can . . . Well, I couldn't let her go on cryin' like that . . . I bet I can find a way all right . . . I bet I can . . . I bet I can fix it up . . . Well,' impatiently, 'I've gotter *think,* haven't I? Gimme time to think . . . I bet I can think of a way. I—'

He stood still in the middle of the road staring in front of him, and the grim expression of his face gave place to one of rapture.

Quite suddenly he had thought of a way. It was so simple that he couldn't imagine why he hadn't thought of it before.

All he had to do was to move the unexploded bomb from the front of Joan's house to the front of Hubert

Lane's house. Then Joan would be able to have her party, and Hubert Lane would not be able to have his. There was an element of poetic justice in the idea that appealed to him strongly. Joan would be able to have her party and Hubert Lane would not be able to have his . . . Even the details of the plan did not seem difficult. He must, of course, wait till no one was about . . . The bomb was not as closely guarded as it had been at the beginning. Even the policeman, whose duty it had been to stand by the barrier, was now generally away on other duties. There was very little traffic on that road in any case, and the inhabitants, once passionately interested in the bomb, had become bored by it and looked on it merely as a nuisance. Occasionally Mr Leicester still came to gaze at it tenderly over the barrier, his eyes gleaming with the pride of possession. His bomb, his beloved unexploded bomb . . . It justified, he felt, his whole career as a warden, gave his life meaning and purpose and inspiration . . .

William realised, of course, that the thing might go off as he was removing it to Hubert Lane's house, but he considered himself quite capable of dealing with that. A saucepan on his head, a tin tray in readiness to use as a shield . . . and then, he thought, the bomb might do its worst. It was too large for him to carry, so he decided to take his ancient and battered soap box on wheels, which was his ordinary means of conveyance and which served regularly the purposes of train, motor car, highwayman's horse or pirate ship as needed in the Outlaws' games . . . He would wait till the coast was clear, make his way down the crater, lift the unexploded bomb into the wooden cart, trundle it down the road to the Lanes' house and leave it there. The policeman or Mr Leicester would soon find it, evacuate the Lanes, bring Joan and her mother back from Miss Milton's and – all would be well. Hubert would not be able to have his party and Joan would be able to have hers . . .

He waited till dusk, put saucepan, tray and spade into his wooden cart and wheeled it off down the road to the barrier outside what had been the Hall gates. The road was empty. The crater lay invitingly easy of access in front of him, with the 'unexploded bomb' in the centre. He glanced around, put the saucepan on his head, slipped under the barrier and climbed down into the crater. He dug carefully all round the bomb. It was bigger than he had thought it would be. It was different altogether from what he had thought it would be . . . He scraped the earth off the top and began to loosen the earth around it. So intent was he on his task that he was unaware of Mr Leicester's approach till he heard a shout and turned to see Mr Leicester hanging over the barrier, his face crimson with rage, his eyes bulging . . .

'Come back!' he shouted hoarsely. 'Come *back*! You – you – you—' Words failed him. His mouth worked soundlessly in his purple face.

William straightened himself and looked from the bomb to Mr Leicester . . . from Mr Leicester to the bomb . . .

'Come *back*!' said Mr Leicester again. His voice was little more than a whisper, but it held even more fury than when it had been a shout.

'COME BACK!' MR LEICESTER SHOUTED HOARSELY. 'COME BACK! YOU – YOU – YOU—' WORDS FAILED HIM.

William wiped his hands down his trousers.

'I'm all right,' he said carelessly. 'I'll fetch my tray thing if it starts explodin' . . . But, I say, it's a jolly funny bomb. Come down an' have a look at it.'

Mr Leicester's eyes, bulging and bloodshot with emotion, went from William to the bomb . . . and remained fixed on it. William had cleared all the earth and debris away from it, and it lay there – large, round, of a greyish hue . . .

Suddenly William gave a shout.

'*Gosh!* I know what it is,' he said.

In the same moment Mr Leicester knew what it was, too.

It was the stone ball from the top of one of the brick piers that had formed the entrance gates of the Hall.

Pale now, but with his eyes still bulging, Mr Leicester dived under the barrier and came down to join William in the crater. He stared at the bomb, stroked it, prodded it . . . His face was a mask of incredulous horror.

'It *is,* isn't it?' said William.

Slowly Mr Leicester turned to him. With an almost superhuman effort he had recovered something of his self-possession, something even of his normal manner. He looked shaken but master of himself.

'No need to – er – go about talking of this, my boy,' he said. 'No need to mention it at all. It would, in fact, be very wrong to – go about upsetting people's morale by – er – spreading rumours. There are very severe penalties for spreading rumours. I hope that you will remember that.'

William looked at him in silence for a few moments. He was an intelligent boy and knew all about the process of face-saving. He was quite willing to help Mr Leicester save his face, but he didn't see why he should do it for nothing.

'Then Joan an' her mother can go home tomorrow?' he said.

'Certainly,' said Mr Leicester graciously.

His eyes kept returning, as if drawn against his will, to the round smooth object at his feet.

'An' you'll come an' give your cinema show at her party, won't you?' said William with elaborate carelessness.

Mr Leicester fixed a stern eye on him.

'You know quite well that I am not giving any such entertainments during the war,' he said.

William gazed dreamily into the distance.

'I thought that if we had the cinema at the party,' he said dreamily, 'it'd be easier for me not to spread rumours.'

Mr Leicester gulped and swallowed. He looked long and hard at William. William continued to gaze dreamily into the distance. There was a silence . . . then Mr Leicester yielded to the inevitable.

'Well, well, my boy,' he said with a fairly good imitation of his pre-war geniality. 'I – er – like to see young people enjoying themselves. If my duties permit, I will make an exception to my rule for this one occasion.'

'An' if they don't,' said William suavely, 'we'll come an' fetch it, shall we? Joan's mother can manage it all right.'

Again Mr Leicester gulped and swallowed. Again he yielded to the inevitable.

'Just this once, then, my boy,' he said graciously. 'Just this once. It must never happen again, of course. And I will take for granted that you will not – er – spread rumours.'

'No,' promised William. 'I won't spread rumours.'

William had barely reached Miss Milton's house next morning when Mr Leicester appeared, complete with all his District Warden's regalia. He looked stern and grim and aloof, as befitted one who has an important part to play in his country's destiny.

'I have come to inform you, Mrs Parfitt,' he said portentously, 'that the unexploded bomb has been – er – disposed of, and that you are at liberty to return to your home at your convenience.'

He avoided William's eye as he spoke.

'Oh how lovely!' said Joan. 'Just in time for the party! It *is* in time for the party, isn't it, Mummy?'

'Yes, dear,' said Mrs Parfitt joyfully. 'It only gives us a day, but we can manage a grand party in a day.'

Mrs Parfitt would have liked to give a dozen parties to celebrate her release from Miss Milton. Only that morning Miss Milton had reproved her for drawing her

'I HAVE COME TO INFORM YOU, MRS PARFITT,' HE SAID
PORTENTOUSLY, 'THAT THE UNEXPLODED BOMB HAS BEEN
– ER – DISPOSED OF.'

bedroom curtains an inch further back on one side than
on the other and had asked her to see that Joan did not
put her hand on the baluster rail going up and down
stairs, as she had found several finger marks on it.

'Ah, yes, the party,' said Mr Leicester with an expan-
sive but somewhat mirthless smile. 'This young man said
that you wanted me to bring my kinematograph to it.'

'Oh *please*, Mr Leicester!' said Joan, clasping her hands and looking up at him beseechingly. 'Oh *please*!'

Mr Leicester gave a good imitation of a strong man melted by a child's pleading.

'Well, well,' he said at last. 'Well, well, well . . . I don't know . . .'

'Oh, *please*!' said Joan again.

'Well,' said Mr Leicester. 'Perhaps . . . just this once . . . Mind, I'll never do it for you again and I'll never do it for anyone else at all – till after the war.'

'That *is* kind of you, Mr Leicester,' said Mrs Parfitt.

Joan was dancing about with joy.

'Oh, won't it be lovely!' she said. 'Oh, *thank* you, Mr Leicester.'

'Isn't it kind of him, William?' said Mrs Parfitt.

'Yes,' agreed William. 'Jolly kind.'

'Er – not at all,' murmured Mr Leicester, fixing his eyes on the air just above William's head. 'Not at all. Don't mention it. An exception, of course . . . Not to be repeated.'

'The bomb didn't explode, then?' said Mrs Parfitt. 'I suppose we'd have heard it here if it had done.'

'Oh no,' said Mr Leicester, repeating the mirthless smile. 'It didn't explode. It was – er – disposed of. The process,' he went on hastily, 'needs specialised knowledge, and the details, I am afraid, are too technical for you to understand.'

Mrs Parfitt looked at him, deeply impressed.

'How fortunate we are to have you for our warden!' she said.

Joan and William walked jauntily down the road, past the Lanes' house. At once Hubert Lane and a few friends, who were in the garden with him, popped their heads over the hedge.

'*Yah!*' they jeered. 'Who's not havin' a party?'

'Well, who isn't?' said William innocently. 'Joan is, an' we're all goin' to it an' we're goin' to have a jolly good time.'

Hubert's mouth dropped open.

'*What!*' he said. 'B-b-b-but what about the bomb?'

'Oh, that!' said William airily. 'Goodness! Fancy you not havin' heard about that! It's been – disposed of. There isn't a bomb there any longer. Joan an' her mother's goin' back home at once.'

Hubert's mouth remained open while he slowly digested this news.

'Well, anyway,' he said, making a not very successful effort to recover himself. 'Anyway, I bet yours won't be such a nice party as ours. I jolly well *bet* it won't.'

'Don't you think so?' said William. He stopped to savour his piece of news before he brought it out. 'Mr

Leicester's comin' to ours an' bringin' his cinema thing an' his films.'

Hubert's eyes goggled. His face paled.

'N-n-n-not Mr Leicester?' he said, as if pleading for mercy. 'N-n-n-not his Mickey Mouse films?'

''Course,' said William cheerfully. 'But he's not goin' to do it for anyone else. Only for Joan . . . Come on, Joan.'

They walked on, leaving a crestfallen silence behind them. Even the Hubert Laneites, pastmasters in the art of jeering, could think of no answering taunt.

As Joan and William walked on down the road, Joan looked suddenly at her companion. He was smiling to himself as at some private joke.

'William,' she said, 'you had *something* to do with it, hadn't you?'

'With what?' said William innocently.

'The bomb and the Mickey Mouse films and – everything.'

'Well, just a bit,' he admitted.

'Oh, William, do tell me.'

He turned to her with a wink.

'I'll tell you after the war,' he promised.

CHAPTER 7

RELUCTANT HEROES

'D'YOU know,' said William thoughtfully at breakfast, 'I don't seem to remember the time there wasn't a war.'

'Don't be ridiculous, William,' said his mother. 'It's hardly lasted two years and you're eleven years old, so you must remember the time when there wasn't a war. All the same,' she added with a sigh, 'I know what you mean.'

Certainly the war seemed to have altered life considerably for William. Sometimes he thought that the advantages and disadvantages cancelled each other out and sometimes he wasn't sure . . . Gamekeepers had been called up and he could trespass in woods and fields with comparative impunity, but, on the other hand, sweets were scarce and cream buns unprocurable. Discipline was relaxed – at school as the result of a gradual infiltration of women teachers, and at home because his father worked overtime at the office and his mother was 'managing' without a cook – but these advantages were offset by a lack of entertainment in general. There were no parties, summer holidays were out of the question because of something called the Income Tax, and for the same reason pocket money, inadequate at the best of times, had faded almost to vanishing point.

Now that Ethel was a V.A.D. and Robert a second lieutenant in one of the less famous regiments, home life had lost much of its friction, but it had also lost something of its zest. William had looked on Ethel and Robert as cruel and vindictive tyrants, but he found, somewhat to his surprise, that he missed both the tyranny and his own plans to circumvent and avenge it.

Even the feud with Hubert Lane lacked its old excitement. There didn't seem to be so many things to quarrel about as there had been before the war. Moreover, William needed a credulous audience for his tales of Robert's prowess and Hubert supplied it. For Robert, in his second lieutenant's uniform, was to William no longer an irascible dictatorial elder brother, hidebound by convention and deaf to the voice of reason. He was a noble and heroic figure, solely responsible for every success the British army had achieved since the war began. It was Robert who had conquered the Italians in Africa, raided the Lofoten Islands, crushed Raschid Ali's revolt . . . Hubert was so credulous that William's stories grew more and more fantastic. It was Robert who, according to William, was solely responsible for the sinking of the *Bismarck*. It was Robert who had captured Rudolf Hess . . . But there even the worm of credulity that was Hubert turned.

'But Robert wasn't in Scotland when Rudolf Hess came over,' he objected.

'How do you know he wasn't?' said William mysteriously. 'Gosh! If I told you the places Robert had been in you wouldn't believe me.'

'Well, there was nothing about him in the papers.'

'No, they kept it out of the papers,' said William. 'Robert's very high up an' everythin' about him's gotter be kept very secret.'

The worm of credulity turned still further.

'Thought he was only a second lieutenant.'

William gave a short laugh.

'They keep him a second lieutenant just to put the Germans off the scent,' he explained, 'so they won't know who it is that's doing all these things.'

'But I bet he didn't capture Rudolf Hess,' persisted Hubert.

'Huh, didn't he!' said William, who was as usual now completely convinced by his own eloquence. 'Well, I can't tell you about it 'cause it's a secret an' I'd get shot if I told people, but it was Robert got him over from Germany to start with.'

'Crumbs!' gasped Hubert.

Hubert, however, though still, in the main, believing William's stories (as I have said, he was an exceptionally credulous boy), was growing a little tired of them. He'd listened to them for weeks on end and the one-sidedness of the situation was beginning to pall. If he'd had a few tales of his own to swap in exchange, he wouldn't have minded so much, but he hadn't. He was an only child and had no elder brother or even near relation to glorify . . . Resentment had been slowly growing in his breast for some time, and the Rudolf Hess story seemed the last straw. He was not a boy to be content to yield the limelight to another indefinitely without becoming restive, and he was now becoming restive. He'd swallowed all Robert's exploits as recounted by William – the African victory, the defeat of Raschid Ali, the sinking of the *Bismarck* . . . He had even swallowed Rudolf Hess, but – he'd reached saturation point.

'What's the matter, Hubert dear?' said his mother solicitously to him at lunch, looking at his plump, sulky face. 'I hope you're not feeling ill, darling.'

'No,' muttered Hubert, 'I'm not feelin' ill. I'm only sick of that ole William Brown.'

Mr Lane shuddered at the name.

'I don't know why you have anything to do with him,'

'WHAT'S THE MATTER, HUBERT DEAR?' SAID HIS MOTHER
SOLICITOUSLY TO HIM AT LUNCH.

Mrs Lane said. Then she turned to her husband. 'Oh, by the way, I heard from Ronald this morning. He's got a week's leave and can spend it with us.'

'Who's Ronald?' said Hubert.

'Didn't I tell you, dear? He's a second cousin of mine. We've never seen much of him because his people always lived in Switzerland. They're still there and so, of course, he can't spend his leave with them and will be very glad to spend it with us . . . I asked him to bring a friend if he liked and he says he'd like to bring another lieutenant in his regiment, who has leave at the same time and has no relations in England to go to. It's rather amusing. He says' – she took a letter out of her pocket, opened it and read – ' "I must warn you that Orford has the most amazing resemblance to Hitler. Actually he takes rather a pride in it, and cultivates the moustache and forelock. So don't think that I've brought Hitler back as a present when you see him." '

Hubert put down his knife and fork and stared open-mouthed at his mother. He didn't often have ideas but he was having one now. It came slowly and painfully, and he turned paler than usual with the unaccustomed effort.

'Darling,' cried Mrs Lane in renewed concern, 'you're not looking at *all* well. Don't you like the pudding?'

'No, I don't like the pudding,' said Hubert calmly. 'It's not sweet enough. But I'm feeling all right 'cept for that.'

*

Hubert walked along the road with a new briskness. There was even a little smile on his face. He looked very pleased with himself. It happened that when he reached the gate of William's house, William himself was coming out of it. They went down the lane together.

'You know, when Robert captured the Hess man,' began William, who had thought out a few more details during lunch, but Hubert interrupted him.

'Funny you should've told me that this morning,' he said.

'Why?' said William.

'Well, it's jus' a sort of coincidence, that's all,' said Hubert.

'What d'you mean, a coincidence?' said William, his curiosity aroused, as Hubert meant it to be.

'Will you promise not to tell anyone?' said Hubert.

'Yes.'

'Cross your throat?'

'Cross my throat.'

'Well, jus' the same sort of thing seems to've happened to a cousin of mine what's comin' to stay with us.'

'The same sort of thing as what?' said William impatiently.

'Same sort of thing as Robert capturin' Hess.'

191

'Dunno what you mean,' said William. 'Your cousin couldn've captured Hess 'cause – I keep tellin' you – Robert captured him.'

'Oh no,' said Hubert, 'he's not captured Hess.' He paused a moment, then brought out with a superb air of casualness: 'He's captured Hitler.'

'*What?*' gasped William, then, recovering himself, said firmly: 'He couldn't have.'

'Why not?' said Hubert, who was enjoying a conversation with William for the first time for weeks.

''Cause he's not been captured.'

'Oh yes, he has,' said Hubert. 'They've not put it in the papers, of course, 'cause it's all gotter be kept secret same as the things Robert does.'

'Well—' William grappled helplessly with the staggering idea. 'Who's carryin' on in Germany then?'

'One of his doubles,' said Hubert. 'He's got dozens of 'em, you know.'

William considered this, frowning thoughtfully.

'I bet this cousin of your mother's pullin' your leg,' he said at last. 'I bet he's not captured him really.'

'Oh yes, he has,' said Hubert confidently.

'Well, you've not got any proof,' persisted William. 'He only *says* he's captured him. I bet he's pullin' your leg.'

Hubert was silent for a few moments, savouring his triumph before he said, still with admirably acted carelessness:

'Oh yes, I've got proof all right. He's bringin' him here today.'

'*What?*' squawked William. Then: 'He *can't* be – I *said* he was pullin' your leg.'

'Yes, he is,' said Hubert. 'The Gov'nment are lettin' him keep him for a bit 'cause they want it kept secret that he's been captured. They don't want the Germans to know what's happened to him an' if they took him prisoner themselves they'd have to put it in the papers. So they're lettin' this cousin of mine keep him for a bit for his own prisoner. He's not dressed like he used to be,' he added hastily. 'He's disguised. He has to be, so's people won't recognise him.'

'Has he got a false beard?' said William, to whom the story was beginning to seem as credible as Robert's exploits, recounted by himself.

'Oh no, he's not got a false beard,' said Hubert. 'That wouldn't be any good. They come off too easy, false beards. No, he's disguised as a British officer same as Robert or this cousin of mine. People'd never think it was Hitler, seein' him in an officer's uniform. An' he's gotter pretend he *is* a British officer, too, an' he's jolly glad to do

193

it 'stead of bein' put in prison. This cousin of mine's taught him English, an' he talks it as well as you or me by now.'

'Gosh!' said William. He took his seat on the top of a stile that led from the lane into a field. 'Come on. Tell us all about it.'

Hubert perched beside him and began the story that he had so carefully prepared on the way.

'Well, it was like this,' he said. 'This cousin of mine was walkin' out in the country one day an' he looked up an' saw a parachute comin' sailin' down from the sky. He ran up to where it landed an' saw it was ole Hitler, an' Hitler said he'd come over same as Hess 'cause ole Goering was after him, so this cousin of mine took him along an' rang up Churchill an' Churchill said: "Well, let's have 'em on toast for a bit wonderin' what's happened to him. Tell you what – s'pose you keep him yourself 'cause if we take him we'll have to put it in the papers. You'd better disguise him as an officer an' teach him English an' take him about with you so's he can't escape." So this cousin of mine did an' when my mother wrote to ask him to spend his leave with us he wrote back to say, yes, he'd like to if he could bring ole Hitler along with him.'

Hubert paused, breathless and exhausted. It was the greatest effort of imagination he had ever made in his life . . . William sat, elbows on knees, chin on hands, gazing into space, considering the story.

'Bet this cousin of yours is pullin' your leg. Bet he'll come alone an' have a good laugh at you for believin' him.'

'All right,' said Hubert. 'He's comin' at six tonight. You come along after that and have a look.'

'Yes, I jolly well will,' said William.

Hubert walked home happily. He had enjoyed the afternoon more than he had enjoyed any afternoon since the war began. It had been a refreshing change to hold forth to William instead of being held forth to by William. It had been a triumph to have concentrated the limelight upon himself instead of watching William enjoy it. It should be quite easy to sustain the Hitler fiction for the few days of his cousin's visit. Fortunately his mother cherished a deep dislike of William as a 'nasty rough boy' and had long ago forbidden him the house.

The excitement with which William had first heard the news decreased slightly as he walked homeward. The cousin had been pulling ole Hubert's leg, of course. Anyone could pull ole Hubert's leg. He'd done it himself dozens of times. He would go round there after tea and he'd bet anyone anything he'd just find ole Hubert's cousin having a good laugh at him.

He waited impatiently till six o'clock, then set off towards the Lanes' house. Not wishing to risk an encounter with Mrs Lane, he concealed himself behind the hedge in a position that gave him a good view of the garden. The garden was empty. No one could be seen at any of the windows of the house.

'Bet the whole thing's a leg-pull,' muttered William. 'Bet he hasn't even got a cousin comin' to stay at all.'

Then the side door opened, and out came Hubert, Mrs Lane and a tall fair man in uniform.

'Hasn't brought a friend at all,' said William. 'Pullin' ole Hubert's leg. I said he was all the time. It's a jolly good joke. I'll have a jolly good laugh at him tomorrow. I'll have a jolly good . . .' His mouth dropped open. His eyes goggled. For at the side door appeared a figure long familiar to him from photographs and caricatures. It was bareheaded. The short moustache, the dark lank forelock, the pallid morose face . . .

'Gosh!' gasped William, going suddenly weak at the knees. '*Gosh!* It's him!'

And, without stopping to consider anything further, he turned to flee as if the whole of the Gestapo were at his heels.

'What on earth's the matter, William?' said his mother as he flung himself, panting and dishevelled, into the

WILLIAM'S MOUTH DROPPED OPEN. HIS EYES GOGGLED.

house a few minutes later, turning to bolt and bar the
front door. 'What *are* you doing that for?'

William gazed at her, still panting. He longed to tell
her the whole story, but he had never yet broken a 'cross
my throat' promise and he wasn't going to start now.
Besides, on thinking the matter over, he decided that there
wasn't really anything to be afraid of. The prisoner was
safely in his captor's hands. Hubert's cousin was presumably armed and would not allow him to escape.

FOR AT THE SIDE DOOR APPEARED A FIGURE LONG
FAMILIAR TO HIM.

'Nothin',' he said. 'Well, nothin' *you* need worry
about. He wouldn't dare start any of his tricks over here.'
'What *are* you talking about, William?'

'Nothin',' said William, drawing back the bolt. 'I bet we'll be all right. I've got my bow an' arrows, anyway, if he does start any tricks.'

He shadowed the illustrious captive from a respectful distance all the next day. The illustrious captive went for a walk with Hubert's cousin in the morning and stayed in the garden in the afternoon. William overheard him commenting on the countryside in excellent English. Certainly Hubert's cousin had done that part of the job successfully. As Hubert had said, he spoke English as well as – or indeed better than – Hubert and William themselves.

The next day the two of them went up to London, and William spent the day in Hubert's company listening to repeated accounts of the capture. Hubert was not gifted with any great imaginative powers and, having with an almost superhuman effort invented the story of the capture, he saw no reason to alter or add to it. William did not exactly become bored – one could hardly be bored by such a story – but he wanted a few more details.

'Well, what's he goin' to do with him next?' he asked.

'Oh, he's just gotter wait till Mr Churchill tells him what to do.'

'Hasn't ole Hitler ever tried to get away?'

'No, he knows he couldn't get away,' said Hubert.

'This cousin of mine'd shoot him soon as look at him if he tried gettin' away.'

'Does he lock him in his room at night or sleep chained to him or what?'

'No,' said Hubert, 'he knows he won't try to get away.'

Despite the undeniable excitement of the situation, there seemed something too static about it for William's taste. It was so fraught with drama that drama should, as it were, spring from it continually.

'Wish he'd try to escape,' he said. 'I bet I'd catch him if he did. He'd be my prisoner then, wouldn't he?'

'Dunno,' said Hubert vaguely, 'but anyway, he won't try. He knows he couldn't get back to Germany an' he quite likes my cousin. He says he reminds him of Gobbles.'

'He's not a bit like Gobbles,' objected William.

'Well, it may be one of the others,' said Hubert, who was finding the whole thing, though enjoyable, something of a tax on his intellect. 'It may be Himmler or Mussolini or someone. Anyway, he says he reminds him of someone. P'raps it was his father . . . I say, you've not told anyone, have you? My cousin'd get in an awful row with Mr Churchill if you've told anyone.'

''Course I haven't,' said William indignantly. 'I said "cross my throat", di'n't I?'

But the keeping of the secret was not proving easy. It hovered on the tip of William's tongue a hundred times a day, though he always managed to choke it back. He decided at last that it could do no harm to hint at the possession of a piece of extraordinary knowledge . . .

'I bet I know somethin' that'd give you a shock if you knew about it, Mother,' he said portentously as he entered the morning-room.

But Mrs Brown had an exciting piece of information of her own to impart.

'I've had a wire today, William,' she said. 'Robert's coming home on leave.'

And that, for the moment, drove the thought of the secret right out of William's head. Robert, the hero, who had conquered Africa, sunk the *Bismarck* and crushed Raschid Ali's revolt . . . William's soul thrilled at the thought of meeting him again.

When Robert actually arrived, however, William found it a little difficult to sustain this attitude. Robert in uniform was so devastatingly like Robert out of uniform – an irascible unreasonable elder brother, passionately interested in such trivial affairs as football results, the fit of his tunic, and the girl friend of the moment. It became more and more difficult to reconcile him with the hero of the sagas that William had so assiduously woven around him.

It wasn't easy even to imagine his capturing Hess . . . But William, born hero-worshipper, was determined to see Robert as he wished to see him. He meant Robert to be a hero, therefore Robert must be a hero. It would have been easier to reconcile oneself to the old unheroic Robert had it not been for Hubert's cousin with his glorious prize just across the way. The more William thought of this, the more intolerable seemed the state of affairs. He would not submit to it. Robert was a hero. Robert should be a hero.

WILLIAM MEANT ROBERT TO BE A HERO, THEREFORE ROBERT *MUST* BE A HERO.

Robert *must* be a hero . . . And yet the situation didn't seem to be one that admitted of heroism. There were not likely to be any more Nazi leaders drifting in parachutes from the skies. It was a pity, thought William regretfully, that Robert had not been there instead of Hubert's cousin when Hitler came down. And then – quite suddenly – William had his idea. It was a stupendous idea. Robert had not captured Hitler, but he could still capture him. There was Hitler under his very nose only about a quarter of a mile away. He could capture him from Hubert's cousin and then he would be his – Robert's – captive, until such time as the Government saw fit to claim him as their own. William, of course, still considered himself bound by his promise. He could not tell Robert in so many words that the Führer was a prisoner at the Lanes' house and ripe for recapture, but he could surely induce the captive to attempt escape and then put Robert on his track. That, though sailing a bit near the wind, wouldn't, he considered, be actually breaking his promise. The scheme called for careful planning. The first thing to do was to get Hitler by himself, and that wouldn't be easy because naturally he spent most of his time in company with his captor.

It was only after a whole day's continuous stalking that William managed to secure his prey. He came upon Lieutenant Orford walking back alone from the village.

Rather apprehensively – for, after all, this was the man who murdered friends and enemies alike by thousands in cold blood, and as it was a lonely stretch of road, William sidled up to him.

'I say,' he said in a conspiratorial whisper, 'why don't you run away?'

Lieutenant Orford stared at him in surprise.

'What on earth are you talking about?' he said.

'There's no one about,' said William. 'I bet you could run away all right.'

Lieutenant Orford waved him impatiently aside and strode on down the road without answering.

William gazed after him regretfully. *That* hadn't been any good. Evidently he didn't want to run away. Scared of being shot, probably . . . He must try to think of some more cunning plan . . . Suddenly he thought of one. He ran to catch up the swiftly moving figure.

'I say!' he panted. 'Hubert's cousin sent a message for you.'

The swiftly striding figure stopped. 'Why on earth couldn't you have said that before?' he snapped.

'Were you expecting a message?' said William cunningly.

''Course I was,' snapped Lieutenant Orford. 'He said that if he'd started before I got back he'd leave a message where he'd gone to.'

'Oh,' said William. 'Well, he's started. He's gone to' – he summoned all his inventive powers – 'he's gone to Poppleham. D'you know where that is?'

'Never heard of it,' said Lieutenant Orford.

'Well, he told me to take you to it if you didn't know it,' said William. 'I don't s'pose you know England very well, do you?'

Lieutenant Orford ignored this remark and they walked on in silence for some moments. Then William said casually:

'I expect you liked it in Germany, di'n't you?'

'Liked what?' said Lieutenant Orford shortly.

'Well, you know, liked it,' said William vaguely, and added after a short pause: 'What d'you think of Hess?'

'I don't think about him at all,' said Lieutenant Orford.

Again conversation flagged. William led his companion over a stile and across a field, breaking the silence finally with: 'I expect they're wonderin' what's happened to you over there.'

'Who?' snapped Lieutenant Orford, 'and over where?'

William sighed. The illustrious captive was evidently determined not to give himself away. Probably he'd made a 'cross my throat' promise not to.

'Oh well,' he said, 'I suppose you don't want people to know about it.'

'Where *is* this Poppleham place?' said Lieutenant Orford irritably.

He was tired of trailing over the countryside with a half-witted child.

'We're nearly there,' said William.

They had reached the old barn now and the next thing was to lure his captive into it.

'I say!' he said, pausing at the open door and peering into the dark corner. 'There's somethin' funny in that corner, isn't there?'

Lieutenant Orford was not devoid of curiosity. He stepped into the barn. William pushed the door to and shot home the bolt.

Robert, seated comfortably in a deck-chair in the garden, looked up at William with a mixture of helplessness and elder-brother severity.

'I don't know *what* you're talking about,' he said shortly.

'Well, I keep *tellin'* you,' persisted William. 'This man came down in a parachute an' he was dressed like a British officer an' he asked me in German where Rudolph Hess was an'—'

'You don't know any German,' objected Robert.

'No, but he translated it into broken English for me an'

I got him to the ole barn an' locked him in. He looked to me sort of as if he might be Hitler, an' I thought it'd be nice for you to take him prisoner.'

'Don't be ridiculous,' said Robert. 'He couldn't *possibly* be Hitler.'

'All right,' shrugged William, 'but he'd got a face like Hitler's an' he came down by a parachute in a British uniform an' started talkin' German.'

'Was it a khaki uniform?'

'Yes.'

'Where's the parachute?'

'Dunno. Think he must have hid it.'

'It's a ridiculous story,' said Robert again, pretending to return to his book.

It sounded ridiculous, of course, but Robert wasn't quite happy about it. Ridiculous things of that sort had happened all over Europe and might happen in England any day, impossible as it still seemed. Suppose there were something in the kid's tale, after all . . . It wouldn't do any harm to verify it. He stood up and closed his book.

'I happen to be going in that direction,' he said loftily. 'You can come along if you like.'

Lieutenant Orford had spent a very uncomfortable quarter of an hour trying to escape from the old barn. It had no windows and, though the door was old, it held firmly. He had kicked and shouted, but no one had heard him. His anger against the half-witted child, who had locked him in had risen to boiling point when suddenly the door opened, revealing the half-witted child in company with a young man. Without stopping to consider, Lieutenant Orford leapt forward to execute vengeance. Robert, for his part, had taken for granted that the whole story was one of William's fantastic inventions. When therefore a figure in khaki, with what in the semi-darkness looked like the face of the German Führer in one of his brain-storms, hurled itself upon them, he lost no time in closing with it. They fought fiercely and silently. Though they were fairly well matched, Robert seemed to be getting the best of it.

'Hold on, Robert!' shouted William. 'I'll go and get a rope.'

It had occurred to him suddenly that it would be a fine score over Hubert if Robert could lead his prisoner past the Lanes' house at the end of a rope . . .

William sat in the wheelbarrow, munching an apple and gazing morosely at the next-door cat, who sat on the fence that divided the gardens, gazing morosely back at William. The adventure had ignominiously petered out to nothing. To worse than nothing . . . for Robert, from being

'HOLD ON, ROBERT!' SHOUTED WILLIAM. 'I'LL GO AND GET
A ROPE.'

super-hero, had become again the old Robert, unheroic
but with a swift sure hand for avenging insults and
injuries, and he had considered that the events of the
afternoon constituted both . . .

It had taken William some time to secure a rope and when he returned to the old barn he had found it empty. He had scoured the countryside for traces of either Robert or his captive, and had then returned home to find the two of them in amicable converse in the morning-room. The visitor had a black eye and Robert a swollen nose. Robert fell upon William without ceremony and it was the visitor who finally rescued him.

'Let the kid off now,' he said. 'It wasn't a bad joke and I thoroughly enjoyed the scrap. It's years since I had a really good one. You're pretty useful with your left, you know.'

'My defence is too slow,' said Robert modestly. 'You were too quick for me. But it was a jolly good scrap.'

It turned out that Robert and Lieutenant Orford had taken to each other. Lieutenant Orford was bored to death with Hubert's cousin and the Lanes. He and Robert were fixing up various dates for the remainder of their leave. They wouldn't even listen to William when he tried to explain what had happened.

'Get *out*!' ordered Robert threateningly.

And William got out.

He munched his apple, continuing to stare morosely at the next-door cat. The next-door cat had, as he knew, troubles of its own. From a diet of sardines, chicken and cream, it had gradually been relegated to skim milk and a nauseous bran-like mixture sold under the misleading name of Cat Food. Meeting William's eye, it opened its mouth in a raven-like croak of disgust.

'Huh!' said William through a mouthful of apple. 'It's all right for *you*. *You've* not had your leg pulled by Hubert Lane.'

The cat eyed him sardonically and repeated its raven-like croak.

'An' been half killed on top of it,' continued William. 'Gosh! I'm sorry for those Germans when Robert gets at 'em.'

He aimed his apple core at the cat. It missed it by several feet.

'Can't even hit a cat,' he continued dejectedly.

The cat uttered what sounded like a sardonic chuckle.

William sank back again into the wheelbarrow and took another apple out of his pocket.

'You're right,' he agreed as he bit into it. 'It's a rotten war.'

CHAPTER 8

WILLIAM AND THE MOCK INVASION

GENERAL Moult, wearing his Home Guard uniform, surveyed the small group of children whom he had summoned from the village and who were sitting on the floor and window-seat of his study.

General Moult had first seen service in the South African war, and his study was a South African museum in miniature. Native weapons, interspersed with mounted horns of various types of antelope, covered the walls. A small chair was upholstered with a lion skin. An elephant's foot formed a waste-paper basket. A hoof of the General's favourite charger had been converted into an ink pot. A highly polished shell of ancient pattern did service as a letter weight. An enlarged photograph of a group of officers – showing the General, youthful, gallant-looking and generously moustached – was ingeniously framed in elephants' tusks. An enormous ostrich egg in a leather case with open doors stood on a book-case filled with books that dealt exclusively with the history, politics, flora and fauna of South Africa.

William and the Mock Invasion

For the first two years of the present war the General, despite his Home Guard duties, had continued to regard it as an insignificant skirmish, but the forthcoming 'mock invasion' seemed to have jerked him out of his rut. He had become so active and energetic and enthusiastic as to be almost an embarrassment to his fellow officers.

'We must leave nothing to chance,' he said, twirling his white moustache belligerently. 'I remember in the battle of Spion Kop . . .'

And now, on the eve of the 'invasion', he had gathered together the junior inhabitants of the village – between the ages of ten and thirteen – and was giving them what he called their 'orders for the day'.

Their eyes roamed round the trophies, growing wider and wider, resting finally, at their widest, on the ostrich egg.

'You children,' the General was saying, 'are, of course, too young to join the Home Guard cadets, but that does not mean that you can do nothing to help in this invasion exercise. No child is too young to help his country. You must all try to do something to harass the enemy and assist the defending forces. Now I can't tell you what to do. Only circumstances can do that. But you must all try to take some active part in it, as far as you can. The enemy will be represented by regular soldiers, and the Home Guard, of course, will be the defenders. We'll have another meeting when it's all over, and I will ask each of you what you have done to help the defending force or hinder the enemy. I have decided to give the ostrich egg you see on the book-case as a prize to the child who has done most.'

Again their gaze turned to the ostrich egg, and they stared at it, open mouthed, hardly able to believe that they had heard aright. The ostrich *egg*! The *ostrich* egg! It seemed impossible that one of them should actually possess the treasure.

'Bet I get it,' muttered Hubert Lane.

They were unusually silent as they walked home. Each was living in a dream in which they captured paratroops, encircled whole divisions . . . won the ostrich egg . . .

'Bet I get it,' muttered Hubert Lane, again. 'Bet you anythin' I get it. I'm jolly good at tricks.'

'Bet you don't,' said William. 'I can do a few tricks myself.'

'Huh!' snorted Hubert.

'Huh!' retorted William.

The next day, Sunday, was the day of the 'mock invasion'. Members of the Home Guard manned machine-guns in the ditches, and soldiers crept behind hedges with rifles in their hands . . . William, filled with enthusiasm, tried to trip up a soldier and was soundly cuffed for his pains. He took part of his own dinner to a Home Guard manning a machine-gun near his home, only to have it thrown into the ditch with a 'I know *that* trick. Read about it in the papers. You'll say I've been poisoned . . .'

The day wore on and William became more and more depressed. No one seemed to want his help. He even tried to 'immobilise' a soldier's bicycle by means of a pin but was caught, pin in hand, by the owner, from whose vengeance he narrowly escaped, as it seemed to him, with his life. He offered to help a Home Guard with his machine-gun but was told to go to blazes. To make things worse he met Hubert Lane, smiling smugly, at the corner of the road.

WILLIAM RAN INTO HUBERT LANE AT THE CORNER OF THE ROAD.

'Gen'ral Moult sent round to ask me for some maps of the district,' said Hubert. 'My father's got ten and I sent 'em all. I bet I get that egg.'

William walked gloomily homeward . . . but at his gate he ran into a young man, who said breathlessly:

'General Moult's sent me to get any maps of the district you have. Hurry up. He wants them at once.'

William brightened. Robert was an enthusiastic motor-cyclist and had a large collection of maps . . . He ran upstairs to Robert's bedroom and opened the top drawer of his bureau . . . Yes, there it was – a long flat cardboard box with 'Motoring Maps' written on the outside. He had often seen Robert taking maps from it or putting them back. William had been forbidden to touch it, but even Robert surely would want General Moult to have it in this crisis. He put it under his arm and ran down to the young man, who was still waiting by the gate.

'Here they are!' he panted. 'I don't know how many there are.'

'Thanks,' said the young man and cycled off with the box under his arm.

William went slowly in to tea. He wished he'd opened the box and counted the maps. He'd like to know whether he'd given more than Hubert Lane. Anyway, he'd *given* them, and that was a weight off his mind. Ole Hubert Lane had nothing on him now. But, as he munched his way through the thick slices of bread and margarine that formed his war-time tea, a vague and ominous memory began to haunt his mind. Had Robert, in those days of tension following Dunkirk when a real invasion was hourly expected, said something about having hidden his maps? The vague memory grew clearer. Robert *had* said something about having hidden his maps . . . Cramming the last piece of bread and margarine hastily into his mouth, he went upstairs to Robert's bedroom. If Robert's maps were hidden, they must be hidden somewhere in his bedroom. An exhaustive search – whose effects nearly gave his mother a heart attack when she entered the room the next morning – at first revealed nothing, and William began to hope that they were, after all, in the box that he had given to General Moult's messenger. Then, idly and no longer really expecting to find them, he took up the paper that covered the bottom of Robert's wardrobe.

There they were laid neatly out beneath it! His mouth dropped open in dismay. Gosh! He'd sent an empty box to General Moult and no maps at all. And Hubert Lane had sent ten. *Gosh!* He must find the young man at once and give him the maps. There was not a moment to be lost. Bundling them into his pocket, he ran downstairs and out into the road. There he looked anxiously up and down but saw no

sign of the young man. He scoured the village and country-side, falling over stiles and scrambling through hedges in his haste, but still found no trace of the young man. His heart was now a leaden weight in the pit of his stomach. It wasn't so much the loss of the ostrich egg he minded, though he did mind that. It was the thought that he had failed his country in its hour of need, for William's vivid imagination had by now transformed the 'mock' invasion into a real one. His search for the young man brought him to the old barn. Passing it, he heard the sound of voices inside and peeped cautiously round the half-open door. General Moult and several other officers were sitting on packing-cases. It was evidently the headquarters of the Home Guard. At least, thought William, he could explain what had happened.

WILLIAM'S MOUTH DROPPED OPEN IN DISMAY.

He entered the barn and approached the group of officers. 'I say!' he began.

General Moult looked up and glared ferociously. All the
others looked up and glared ferociously.

Someone said '*Get* out!' William, stumbling over a
packing-case, got out . . .

He went home, to find the maps no longer in his pocket.
Somewhere in his scrambling over stiles and through hedges

he must have lost them. Practically *given* them to the enemy – for it would be just his luck if a soldier and not a Home Guard found them. Gosh! Fate just seemed to have a down on him . . . Well, he couldn't leave things in the mess they were in. He must do *something* to retrieve the position. Then – quite suddenly – the idea came to him. Commandos. Why shouldn't there be Commandos in the invasion? Probably just because no one had thought of it. The Home Guard surely ought to have a few Commandos to help it. He'd be a Commando . . . It only needed a tin of blacking and a pair of bedroom slippers. He could easily get both. He proceeded to do so. It was the work of a few moments to abstract a tin of boot blacking from the kitchen, plaster his face with it, and put on his bedroom slippers . . . Then he crept in conspiratorial fashion from the house . . . It was unfortunate that he met Violet Elizabeth Bott at the gate. She gave a cry of delight when she saw him.

'Oh, William, you *do* look funny! What are you playing at?'

'I'm not playing at anythin',' said William sternly. 'I'm a Commando in the invasion. Go away. I don't want you messing round.'

'Can't I play, too, William?' pleaded Violet Elizabeth. 'I like funny gameth.'

'It's *not* a game,' repeated William.

'OH, WILLIAM, YOU *DO* LOOK FUNNY!' CRIED VIOLET
ELIZABETH.

'Have you any more black thtuff?' said Violet Elizabeth.
It turned out that William had. He had put the tin
into his pocket in case he had to renew his make-up
during the course of the evening. Reluctantly he brought
it out. Morosely he watched Violet Elizabeth plaster her
small face with it.

'Now I'm all black, too,' she said happily. 'What thall we
play at?'

'I keep tellin' you, I'm not playin' at anythin',' said
William impatiently. 'I'm helpin' conquer the Germans.'

221

'I'm thick of the Germanth,' pouted Violet Elizabeth. 'Leth pretend we're explorerth.'

'I tell you I'm a Commando,' said William, 'an' girls can't be them. They're too soppy.'

'Girlth *aren't* thoppy, William,' said Violet Elizabeth, stung by this insult to her sex. 'I don't thee why they thouldn't be Commandoth thame ath the Atth and Waacth and Wrenth. I'm going to be one, anyway, and you can't thtop me. I'm going to be a Waac. That meanth Women Auxiliary Commando. Girlth *aren't* thoppy, William. I'm going to be a Waac an' *help* you, thame ath the otherth do.'

'It means goin' into danger – p'raps death,' said William darkly.

'I don't mind,' said Violet Elizabeth, dismissing death and danger with an airy gesture. 'It'th a nithe game.'

'I keep *tellin'* you it's not a game,' snapped William. 'I'm in earnest.'

'All right,' said Violet Elizabeth serenely, 'I don't mind. I'll be in earnetht, too.'

William sighed and yielded to the inevitable. He had tried to shake off Violet Elizabeth before and knew that it could not be done. After all, she would afford him a spectator for his exploits, and William liked to have a spectator for his exploits . . .

He walked down the lane, Violet Elizabeth trotting beside him.

'Let'th play at being Robinthon Cruthoe and Friday,' she suggested brightly.

William did not deign to answer.

'Well, let'th pretend we're ecthplorerth, then,' she said. 'It'th tho dull jutht being Commandoth.'

'You wait,' said William. 'You wait till I get going.'

'All right. What do we do firtht?'

'Well – er – I'll climb a tree and have a good look round for sentries, then I'll creep up behind 'em and kill 'em.'

'But I like thentrieth,' objected Violet Elizabeth. 'They're nithe.'

'Well, I don't want you, anyway, an' I wish you'd go away . . . I'm goin' to go into this field an' climb this tree.'

'Can I climb it, too?'

'No.'

'All right. I don't mind. I alwayth get thtuck in treeth.'

William went across the field to a large oak tree that grew by the farther hedge. He had often climbed it before and took only a few seconds to reach a good vantage point about half-way up. Violet Elizabeth waited patiently till he rejoined her.

'I got a jolly good view,' he said excitedly. 'I could see two men in khaki, guardin' things. One was guardin' the telephone box by the road an' the other was guardin' the bridge over the river. I could jump down on both of 'em an' overpower them, but I can't tell from here which is ours an' which is the enemy. I say! You go round an' find out which is which. See which of 'em's a reg'lar soldier an' which is a Home Guard. P'raps,' hopefully, 'they're both reg'lar soldiers an' I can overpower both of 'em. Anyway, it's no good lettin' them see me before I start overpowerin' them or it'll put 'em on their guard. You go first an' find out which is which an' come back an' tell me an' then I'll go an' overpower whichever's the enemy.'

'All right,' agreed Violet Elizabeth and trotted off obediently.

William meantime searched for suitable weapons in the neighbouring hedge. He found a short stout stick with which, he thought, he could stun his opponent, and his pocket already contained a length of string with which he hoped to secure his victim when stunned.

Violet Elizabeth soon came trotting back

'The one by the bridge ith a Home Guard, William,' she said, 'an' the one by the telephone booth ith a reg'lar tholdier.'

'All right,' said William. 'I'll overpower the one by the telephone box.'

'Can I come, too?' asked Violet Elizabeth.

'No,' said William firmly. 'I'm goin' into deadly danger an' it's no place for women. Besides, you always mess things up.'

'All right, William,' said Violet Elizabeth with unexpected docility. 'I'll wait for you here.'

William crept across the field to the point in the road where the telephone box was. Carefully, silently, with the help of some railings at the side of the road, he climbed up to the top of the telephone box, then peeped cautiously over the top. All he could see was a netted tin hat, a khaki battle dress and an enormous pair of boots. The best way to overpower the enemy was, he had decided, to fling himself down upon him from above and, while the enemy was still bewildered, stun and bind him . . .

He waited breathlessly for a few seconds. Evidently the enemy, leaning against the telephone box in an attitude of extreme boredom, had not heard his approach. William set his teeth and drew a deep breath . . . One, two, three . . .

For a few seconds William and the khaki-clad figure rolled about the road in indistinguishable confusion. Unfortunately the figure in khaki recovered first from his confusion, dragged William to his feet and boxed his ears.

'You little devil, you!'

'Listen!' said William, rubbing his head, which had felt the full impact, first of the warrior's tin hat and then of his

WILLIAM LOOKED CAUTIOUSLY OVER THE TOP OF THE
TELEPHONE BOX.

large and horny hand. 'Listen! You don't understand. I'm a Commando an' I've captured you. At least, I dropped my stick when I fell off, but, if I'd got my stick, I'd've captured you, so—' he broke off, staring in amazement at the warrior's sleeve. 'Gosh! You're a Home Guard!'

''Course I'm a Home Guard,' snapped the warrior. 'And, let me tell you, you can get into serious trouble for interfering with a Home Guard in the pursuit of his duties. You may not know that this is an invasion practice, and that I'm guarding vital communications. I don't suppose you even know there's a war on. I suppose you think of nothing but your inane monkey tricks. Boys like you are a menace to the community . . .'

'Listen,' pleaded William again. 'I was tryin' to help. I—'

But the Home Guard advanced upon him threateningly.

'Go home,' he said. 'Go home and wash your face.'

William, in no condition to venture upon further hostilities, took ignominiously to flight.

He found Violet Elizabeth sitting under the tree where he had left her, sucking a piece of chocolate.

'Look here!' William accused her indignantly. 'You made me attack the wrong side. He wasn't a reg'lar soldier.'

'I know he wathn't,' agreed Violet Elizabeth, mildly apologetic, 'but I wath playing a *different* game – a game of my own. I wath pretending I wath an ecthplorer, theeing which were the friendly tribeth and the one by the bridge wath *a very* friendly one. He gave me a thlab of chocolate and I didn't want you to kill him, cauthe he wath tho nithe and kind, but the one by the telephone booth wath very dithagreeable and wouldn't even thpeak to me, tho I wanted you to kill him, cauthe he wath tho croth. That'th why I told you he wath a reg'lar tholdier, cauthe I wanted you to kill him. He detherved to be killed for being tho nathty and croth.'

William was beyond even remonstrance. He dug his hands into his pockets and trailed dejectedly homewards.

He was tempted not to attend the meeting at General Moult's house the next morning. He had nothing to offer but a record of failure and disgrace that would expose him to the triumphant jeering of his enemies for months to come. He hadn't even contributed a single map, and his encounter with the Home Guard was still a painful memory. It seemed, however, cowardly to shirk it, so, sore in both mind and body, he set out for the meeting.

Hubert Lane and his friends were already there, grinning complacently. They had all sent maps, and one of them, Hubert probably, would be sure to get the prize. William took his seat at the end of the row, his freckled face set and scowling. The ostrich egg still stood on the top of the book-case. It seemed to regard him with mingled derision and contempt.

'How many maps did you send the General, William?' said Hubert, and his friends sniggered in appreciation of the taunt.

General Moult entered and took his seat at his writing-desk.

'Now I'll ask you children, one by one, what you did yesterday to help the defending forces,' he said. 'I'll ask Hubert Lane first.'

Hubert smirked triumphantly.

'I sent you ten maps,' he said, 'an' I bet no one else sent as many as that. My dad's always buying new maps. He buys jolly expensive ones, too.'

General Moult passed on to the next without comment.

'I sent you three maps.'

'I sent you four maps.'

'I only sent one, but it was a jolly good one.'

Hubert sat with his eyes fixed gloatingly on the ostrich egg. He would put it in the hall where everyone would see it as they came into the house, and he would tell everyone how he'd won it. If he wasn't in, his mother would tell them. No one had sent more than ten maps. He was sure of the prize. He'd scored over ole William Brown at last, and he wouldn't let him forget it in a hurry.

'And what about you, William Brown?' the General was saying.

William tried not to see Hubert's jeering face. He gulped and swallowed miserably.

'I tried to knock out one of the invaders,' he said, 'but – but I got a Home Guard by mistake.'

The General waved this aside.

'No real harm done,' he said, 'or I'd have heard of it.' He cleared his throat and addressed his audience. 'All you children, except one, have fallen into a trap. The man who came round asking for maps and purporting to have come from me was a fifth columnist. His aim was to procure maps for

'AND WHAT ABOUT YOU, WILLIAM BROWN?' ASKED THE GENERAL.

the invaders and deplete the supply of maps available for the defenders. Only one of you tumbled to the fact that it might be a trick. That boy – realising, of course, that to refuse outright would be dangerous – very cunningly gave the man an empty box labelled "Maps" then, just in case the message was a genuine one, brought the maps round to me at Headquarters.' William gasped. The maps must have fallen out of his pocket when he tumbled over the packing-case in the old barn. 'I'm afraid I was rather abrupt on that occasion, as I did not realise the object of the boy's visit, but I congratulate you on your intelligence, William Brown, and have much pleasure in presenting you with the prize.'

Dazedly William rose to his feet. Dazedly he murmured thanks. Dazedly he took the precious case under his arm . . .

Violet Elizabeth accompanied him homeward, smiling radiantly.

'I helped you win it, didn't I, William?' she said. 'It wath me that won it really, wathn't it, by helping you overpower that dithagreeable man that didn't give me any chocolate.'

And he was too dazed even to contradict her.

231

CHAPTER 9

WILLIAM AND THE TEA-CAKE

IF it hadn't been for Mrs Mason, no one in the village would have taken any notice of Fräulein Schmitt, or Miss Smith, as she preferred to be called. Miss Smith was an Austrian refugee, who had come to the Vicarage as a 'help' about a year before the war – small, shy, timid and quiveringly anxious to justify her position. Moreover, her admiration of everything British was so extreme as to be almost embarrassing.

'Your calmness, your courage, your kindness,' she would say, hands clasped, pale eyes brimming with tears, 'they are an amazement to me. Constantly they are an amazement. Never in all my life have I been so happy as I am among you. After all my suffering it is like reaching haven after storm. My gratitude overwhelms me. Never do I wish to leave this beautiful country, these kind brave people. Here is my spiritual home.'

The recipients of these compliments felt vaguely flattered but were, generally speaking, too busy to do anything about it beyond greeting her kindly when they met her scurrying about the village on her patriotic activities. These consisted chiefly of knitting innumerable sea-boot stockings and helping at the local canteen that was patronised by large numbers of the airmen from Marleigh Aerodrome. Mrs Monks, her employer, gave her every afternoon 'off', and Miss Smith spent them all at the canteen. It was difficult to get helpers for the afternoon shift, so Miss Smith took it on every day. She said that it was a small way of repaying all the kindness she had received in her beloved adopted country . . . She never wanted to go anywhere else or do anything else and she had no friends. She kept the Vicarage in perfect order and cooked succulent meals out of nothing at all. Mrs Monks called her a 'treasure' and left it at that. It wasn't till Mrs Mason came to the village that the limelight began to fall upon Miss Smith.

Mrs Mason's journalistic genius had so far functioned chiefly in the atmosphere of Bloomsbury, but removal to the country seemed to have given it fresh impetus, and after a week or two, having exhausted every other topic connected with the village, she fell upon Miss Smith, the Grateful Refugee. Mrs Mason pursued her indefatigably, interviewing her on her sufferings in her native land and on those feelings of gratitude to her adopted country that found such constant outlet in sea-boot stockings and the local canteen. And then – when one would have thought that she had said all that could possibly be said on the subject – she discovered Miss Smith's soldier. Miss Smith's soldier was a tall stooping military-looking man, with a white moustache and a limp, who had moved from London at the beginning of the war and lived in rooms in Hadley. He took a 'constitutional' into the country every afternoon, walking slowly and leaning heavily on his stick, and, passing the canteen, would often go in for a rest before continuing his walk. And Miss Smith adopted him. He became her soldier. He was a silent reserved man, but questioning would draw from him an account of how he had been gassed and shot through the spine in the last war . . . and to Miss Smith he typified all the other soldiers who had suffered these things for her freedom. Moreover, he had been a prisoner of war in Germany and could speak a little German, which he practised with shy pride upon Miss Smith. Miss Smith discovered that he had been born in Yorkshire and that one of his happiest memories was the Yorkshire tea-cakes that his mother used to make . . . He had never tasted anything to compare with them, he said, since he came South . . . So, in order to give him a pleasant surprise, Miss Smith set to work to make a Yorkshire tea-cake. She hunted through recipe books; she experimented on the Vicarage gas cooker . . . till she had at last made a Yorkshire tea-cake that she considered fit to be offered to him. And he pronounced it good – as good, in fact, as the tea-cakes his mother used to make. Miss Smith's gratification was unbounded, and thereafter, whenever the soldier stopped at the canteen, Miss Smith would have a tea-cake ready for him to take home with him. Mrs Mason seized on the story with zest and wrote an article – Fräulein Schmitt, the Soldier and the Tea-cakes – which appeared in one of the monthly reviews. After that, having exhausted every other subject, she took refuge in those happy hunting grounds of the journalist – War-time Cookery and The Mistakes Our Generals Have Made in Every Theatre of the War – and Miss Smith relapsed into oblivion.

Not entirely into oblivion, however, for the story of the tea-cake had somehow struck the popular imagination. Even Mrs Brown, harassed as she was by points and coupons, by the curious appearance of war-time sausages and the still more curious disappearance of war-time eggs, found time to turn up an old cookery book and make a Yorkshire tea-cake.

'I think it's quite a success,' she said modestly. 'Anyway, will you take it down to the canteen for me, William. It's the day her soldier generally calls, I believe. I don't suppose it's as good as Miss Smith's, but tell Miss Smith that

I'd like him to have it as well as hers, just to see if it's all right. If it is, I could make one or two occasionally to save her the trouble.'

William had arranged to play in the woods with Ginger that afternoon, but, like everyone else in the village, he felt a proprietary pride in Miss Smith and her soldier, so he took the paper bag his mother gave him and set off for the Church Room, where the canteen was held. He found Miss Smith arranging cakes and teacups on long trestle tables.

'Mother sent you this for your soldier,' said William, taking the tea-cake out of the bag and putting it on the table.

Miss Smith clasped her hands in ecstasy.

'But you are so kind,' she said. 'You are all so kind. I am so grateful, and my soldier, he will be so grateful, too. I will put it here, next to the one I have made myself, and he shall have them both. I am so glad to be here to give your kind mother's tea-cake to my friend. We have been doing what you call the spring cleaning at the Vicarage, and I had almost decided not to come this afternoon, as we had reached the stairs, which, as you doubtless know, is in spring cleaning a most difficult point, but dear Mrs Monks insisted that I should have my usual time off this afternoon. "Send for me," I said, "should any crisis occur and I will close the canteen and come." She said she could manage perfectly, so I came.'

William was on the point of taking his departure, when the small boy who represented the outdoor staff of the Vicarage appeared in the doorway.

'Please, Miss Smith, Mrs Monks says she's very sorry to trouble you, after all, but could you come just a minute to give her a hand with the stair carpet? She's puttin' of it back an' got to the bend an' she says it's a bit tricky an' she says I'm not big enough to help an' she says could you close the canteen or get someone to leave in charge just for a few minutes an' she's very sorry to trouble you.'

The small boy paused for breath.

'Oh dear!' said Miss Smith, looking more put out than this simple message warranted. 'Of course I will come at once. I do not like to close the canteen. It is true that few people come to the canteen at this so early hour, but I do not like that those who do should find a closed door.' Her eye fell speculatively upon William. 'I wonder . . . I will not be away long, dear boy, and few will come. Perhaps you would be kind to – what you say – hold the fort? No one will want more than a cup of tea and a cake. You can pour out a cup of tea from the teapot which I have freshly made, and the cakes are all on the plates set out. The cups of tea are a penny and the cakes are twopence . . . And, of

'WILL YOU HOLD THE FORT, DEAR BOY?' ASKED MISS SMITH.

course, should my soldier come, this is the cake I have made for him.' She took a paper bag from the shelf above the sink, opened it and showed a round tea-cake, floury and nicely browned. 'You will give it to him, will you not, my dear boy? Of course I may be back before he comes . . . I thank you, my dear boy, so kind and good and helpful, like all the boys of your beloved country.'

With that she scurried away, leaving William to 'hold the fort' . . .

William and the Tea-cake

For a few minutes, William sat behind the teapot waiting for customers. None came. He began to grow bored. He began to grow hungry. To sit like this, surrounded by plates of buns and cakes – jam rolls, doughnuts, treacle tart, chocolate cake – was, he thought pathetically, an ordeal such as few are called upon to undergo in their country's service. It was an ordeal, however, that he realised he must undergo without flinching. The cakes belonged to the Forces, and to rob the Forces of food was a crime from which his soul shrank in horror. Like one of the saints of old, he sat with his eyes resolutely turned away from temptation – especially from the treacle tart, which was his greatest weakness. But, as his hunger grew, his thoughts began to turn to the tea-cake that his mother had made. No question of patriotism was involved in that. That question lay, not between William and his country, but between William and his mother. Miss Smith's soldier had, of course, fought in the last war, but that was ancient history now, and he had a shrewd idea that Miss Smith's soldier did very well out of Miss Smith. In any case, he would have Miss Smith's tea-cake, which was all he was expecting. He took his mother's tea-cake out of its bag and Miss Smith's tea-cake out of its bag and laid them side by side on the shelf. They looked very much alike. Perhaps one was a little bigger than the other. If he were driven by the pangs of hunger to eat one, he would eat the smaller one, of course . . .

The door opened, and he turned expectantly. A customer or the old soldier? But it was neither. It was Mrs Mason. She entered, smiling coyly and carrying a paper bag in her hand. The smile faded from her face when she saw William.

'I thought Miss Smith would be here,' she said.

'She's had to go to the Vicarage,' explained William, ''cause of the stair carpet bendin', but she won't be long.'

'Has her soldier been yet?' said Mrs Mason.

'No, not yet,' said William.

Mrs Mason opened the paper bag and drew out a tea-cake.

'I've made a tea-cake for him,' she said proudly. 'I'm doing a column of war-time tea-cakes and I've tried them all, and I think this is the best. I'm so sorry Miss Smith isn't here. I'd stay and give it to him myself, but I'm going to Upper Marleigh to interview someone who has a new idea for Post-War Reconstruction – something to do with the Pyramids, I believe. It may, or may not, prove worth writing up. Anyway, here's the tea-cake. Tell him it's from the lady who wrote the article about him and give him my best wishes. And now I must fly. I hope that Miss Smith will be back soon, because I really – *really* – don't think that you are a suitable person to be left in charge of' – she waved her hand around her – 'all this. However . . .'

With that she vanished abruptly.

William took her tea-cake out of its bag and placed it with the others on the shelf. They were all so much alike that he could hardly tell which was which.

The door opened again. This time it was a customer – a despatch rider in crash helmet and leather jerkin who curtly demanded a cup of tea and piece of swiss roll. His heart swelling with pride, William poured out a cup of tea, put a piece of swiss roll on a plate, took the three pennies and dropped them into the till. The despatch rider was a man of few words. Displaying no surprise at seeing a small boy in charge of the canteen, he drank down his cup of tea in three gulps, ate the swiss roll in two mouthfuls, said 'Cheerio' and vanished. The sight of the despatch rider's meal had increased William's hunger. Its pangs had by now become almost unbearable. He turned his eyes away from the treacle tart and fixed them on the three tea-cakes. By this time he hadn't any idea which was which . . . but they looked jolly good . . . After all, one had been made by his mother, and he was certain that, if she knew how hungry he was, she would want him to have it. She could easily make another for Miss Smith's soldier. In fact, the more he thought about it, the more convinced he became that it was his duty to eat it, if only to save himself from the crime of eating the Forces' food. He didn't know, of course, which of the three tea-cakes was his mother's, and he didn't see that it mattered. They were all tea-cakes and surely one was enough for Miss Smith's soldier . . .

He took up the nearest and bit into it. Yes, it was jolly good. He was munching away happily, when suddenly his teeth struck something hard . . . It was a jolly big currant, or could it be a piece of candied peel? He took it out of his mouth. Gosh! It was an India rubber – one of those long ones. *Gosh!* His mother or whoever had made it must have dropped it into the cake by mistake when she was making it. Well, an India rubber was a jolly useful thing to have, and he didn't suppose she'd want it now. He'd take it home and wash it. He slipped it into his pocket and finished the tea-cake . . . Yes, it was *jolly* good! Fortified by it, he could even look at the treacle tart without weakening. He put one of the remaining tea-cakes back into its bag and was just going to put away the other when the door opened again, and an old tramp sidled into the room. He was a picturesque tramp, with a tattered frock coat and a pair of trousers that still showed between rents and patches the remains of a black and white check and might even in days gone by have graced a Victorian wedding. In place of a collar he wore a dingy cotton handkerchief that might once have been red and his boots (he wore no socks) were tied together by string. What could be seen of his face through a covering of grime and several days' growth of beard wore a cheerful good-humoured expression.

''Ullo,' he greeted William. 'Anythin' to eat?'

'It's only for soldiers,' explained William.

'That's orl right,' said the tramp easily, coming into the room and slinging a sort of bundle, tied up in old sacking, from his shoulder. 'I fought in the Boer war *an*' the las' one, so if I'm not a soldier I don't know 'oo is.' His eyes roved round the heaped plates. 'Now wot've you got?'

'You've gotter pay for 'em,' said William.

He tried to speak firmly but sounded weakly apologetic. He knew that tramps were considered undesirable characters and his own experience of them had not been encouraging, but they possessed an irresistible fascination for him. They represented that life of outlawry that had always appealed to him – a life of glorious freedom, unshackled by the trammels of respectability and civilisation. He would have liked to give this satisfying representative of the species the whole roomful of cakes, but he had to account for them to higher powers . . .

'They're not mine,' he added. 'If they were mine I'd give them you, but they're for the Forces.'

'THIS 'ERE LOOKS A BIT OF ORL RIGHT,' SAID THE TRAMP.

William and the Tea-cake

The tramp had drawn a battered leather purse from the recesses of his rags.

'Well, I can pay fer wot I eats, young 'un, same as anyone else. I've bin 'elpin' at a farm over Marleigh way, an' I got me wages.'

'Well, a cup of tea's a penny and the cakes are twopence,' said William.

He looked anxiously at the door as he spoke. He was aware that the presence of this customer in the canteen would not be approved by Authority, and he was eager to do what he could to satisfy him before Authority could intervene.

But the tramp was taking his time . . . wandering down the trestle table, inspecting each plate in turn.

'The treacle tart looks jolly good,' said William.

'Maybe,' said the tramp. 'I'll 'ave a good look round, anyways, an' see wot I fancies . . .' His eye rested on the tea-cake that lay on the trestle table in front of William's chair. 'This 'ere looks a bit of orl right.'

'You can't have that,' said William. 'That's for Miss Smith's soldier.'

'An' 'oo may 'e be?' said the tramp indifferently. 'Well, I jus' fancies that cake an' I don't fancy any of the others. 'Ow much is it?'

'It isn't for sale,' said William.

The tramp shook his head.

'If a cake's displayed 'ere, it's fer sale,' he said stubbornly. 'That's the lor, young 'un. You can't refuse money fer somethin' wot's displayed fer sale same as this 'ere cake is, an' I've took a fancy to it. It's bigger than the others, an' I'm willin' to pay a bigger price fer it. 'Ow about fourpence?'

'B-but it's not for sale,' said William again.

'Now, young 'un,' said the tramp, 'you can't refuse fourpence fer the funds of this 'ere canteen. Where's yer patriotism? This 'ere Mrs Smith – 'ooever she is – won't grudge fourpence to a war he'ffort like this 'ere, nor will 'er soldier – 'ooever 'e is. Not if they've got any patriotism. Mind you, fourpence is fourpence an' everyone wouldn't give it you fer a cake this size, but I've took a fancy to it. It's a *satisfyin'* lookin' sort of cake, the sort I used to 'ave when I was a child . . . Well, make up yer mind quick, young 'un. If I wos you, I wouldn't like to take the responsibility of turning down a hoffer like this. I don't suppose 'ooever runs this 'ere show'll be pleased when they comes to 'ear of it. You don't get hoffered fourpence fer a cake hevery day.'

William considered. After all, there would be one teacake left, and Miss Smith's soldier was not expecting more than one. To sell one to the tramp would be, as the tramp pointed out, fourpence clear profit to the canteen funds.

'All right,' he said suddenly, 'you can have it.'

'Thanks, young 'un,' said the tramp. 'Now you can 'ave the satisfaction of thinkin' that you've give one of 'is Majesty's ole soldiers a treat *an*' made fourpence for the war heffort . . .' He opened the battered purse, put four pennies down on the trestle table, slipped the cake into his bundle, then slung the bundle over his shoulder again. 'Well, so long, young 'un.'

He shuffled out, stopping at the doorway to light an old clay pipe. William went to the door and watched him wistfully as he took his way over the fields in the direction of Marleigh, his rags fluttering in the breeze. The attractions of every other imaginable career paled in comparison. After all, he considered, brightening, once he was twenty-one, no one could stop him being a tramp if he wanted to . . . Then he returned to the canteen and to the contemplation of his more immediate problems. Had he done right in selling the tea-cake to the tramp? Were the claims of Miss Smith's soldier more important than the claims of the canteen funds? Would he get into trouble if it were found out? Perhaps it never would be found out. Mrs Mason was notoriously absent-minded. It probably depended on whether the Pyramid Post-War Reconstruction Plan proved worthy of being written up . . .

The door opened and Miss Smith's soldier entered, walking slowly and painfully, leaning on his stick.

'Miss Smith not here?' he said, looking round the canteen.

He had a quiet gentle voice that went well with his appearance of neatness and delicacy. There was about him the suggestion of one who had suffered illness and poverty but never lost his self-respect.

'She won't be long,' said William. 'She had to go back to the Vicarage 'cause of the bend in the stair carpet. She left the tea-cake for you.'

The soldier smiled pleasantly at William.

'That's very kind of her,' he said. 'I'm sorry I can't wait to see her. I have to go back to Hadley . . . You'll give her my thanks and grateful regards – won't you? – and tell her how sorry I was not to be able to stay and see her.'

'Yes,' said William, greatly impressed by the courtly bearing of the visitor.

He put the remaining cake into a bag and handed it over the table.

Still smiling pleasantly and drawing himself up for a ceremonious salute, Miss Smith's soldier took his departure.

William felt gratified at having participated in the little drama that had become so famous. His conscience still troubled him about the other two tea-cakes, but again he assured himself that the soldier had only expected one.

The minutes passed . . . Boredom and hunger once more began to claim him, but, before he could yield to either, Miss Smith came trotting into the room, her small face wearing its usual shy, timid, apologetic smile.

'I am so sorry to have left you for so long,' she said. 'It is kind of you to have stayed. The stair carpet proved difficult indeed at the bend, but dear kind Mrs Monks and I have finally mastered it . . . Has my soldier been?'

'Yes,' said William. 'I gave him your cake.'

'That is good,' said Miss Smith with what seemed to be a quick sigh of relief. 'That is indeed good. I should not have liked the poor man to miss his tea-cake . . . Well, my dear boy, I must not keep you longer.' She took an apron from her bag and began to tie it round her waist. 'I suppose you have not had many customers?'

'N-not many,' said William and was wondering how to account for the extra fourpence without revealing that he had disposed of a tea-cake intended for the old soldier, when the door opened and the old soldier himself came in. He looked – different somehow. Less gentle and courteous. Less delicate. Even less old. He began to talk to Miss Smith in German. Miss Smith answered him in German. Miss Smith too seemed different. Less timid, less

THE OLD SOLDIER BEGAN TO TALK TO MISS SMITH IN
GERMAN.

meek . . . but certainly not less anxious. It must be talking
German that made them seem different, thought William.

Then Miss Smith turned to him. She was the old Miss
Smith, but, as it seemed, by an effort.

'You gave this gentleman the tea-cake I gave you for
him, did you not?' she said.

They watched him in silence, and in the silence

William was aware of a curious cold feeling travelling up and down his spine.

'Not *exactly*,' he admitted, deciding to make a clean breast of it. 'I ate the one my mother made an' Mrs Mason brought another an' I sold it to an ole tramp for fourpence. You see, I thought—'

'Which way did he go?' cut in the soldier sharply, and again that curious cold shiver crept up and down William's spine.

'Up the field path towards Marleigh,' said William.

'You little—' began the soldier fiercely, but Miss Smith shook her head at him warningly and turned to William with a graciousness and geniality that were somehow more terrifying than that momentary glimpse of anger had been.

'You have been so kind, dear boy, will you be even more kind and stay here while I and my friend just – er – return to the Vicarage to give Mrs Monks a little further help? It will not take long with the two of us and we will be back soon. Goodbye for the present.'

They had vanished before William could answer. He stood for a few moments considering the situation. He felt bewildered – so much bewildered that he could even look at the treacle tart with no other emotion than bewilderment . . . He went to the door and looked down the road towards the Vicarage. It was empty. He looked up the

WILLIAM WENT TO THE DOOR AND LOOKED DOWN THE
ROAD TOWARDS THE VICARAGE.

fields towards Marleigh. Yes, there were Miss Smith and
her soldier . . . They were walking quickly. Miss Smith's
soldier didn't seem lame any more. They had almost
reached the old barn. He returned to the canteen more
bewildered than ever and gazed unseeingly at the dainties
around him. His bewilderment, he felt, was natural. What
surprised him was that curious feeling of fear that still
possessed him. How *could* he be afraid of sweet timid
little Miss Smith and her gentle old soldier? But the fact

MISS SMITH AND HER SOLDIER HAD ALMOST REACHED THE OLD BARN.

remained that he had been and still was. Anyway, why were they going up the hill towards Marleigh, obviously following the tramp, when Miss Smith had plainly said that they were going to the Vicarage?

On an impulse William went out, closing the door behind him, and set off across the fields. There were no signs of the tramp, Miss Smith or Miss Smith's soldier. He was just passing the old barn when he thought he heard voices inside. He stopped. The door was shut, but there was a crack in it, and he approached cautiously, applying his eye to the crack . . . At first he could hardly believe what he saw. The tramp was cowering in a corner of the barn and over him stood Miss Smith and her soldier. The soldier was only just recognisable. His face was set in lines that sent that shiver again up and down William's spine. And on Miss Smith's face, too, was a reflection of the cold savagery that had so transformed her soldier's.

'What have you done with it?' the soldier was saying.

'I dunno wot yer mean, guv'ner,' whined the tramp. 'I ain't done nuffin'. I ain't took nuffin'. You ain't got no right ter knock me abaht like this 'ere. I paid the little varmint fourpence fer me cake, I did. I can't 'elp it if 'e didn't oughter've sold it me. I've et it, I tell you. I can't give it you back.'

'You know what I mean,' said the soldier. 'What have you done with it?'

'Give him something else to refresh his memory,' said Miss Smith in that low vicious tone that was not Miss Smith's at all.

The soldier raised his fist and the tramp cowered down before him, whimpering, putting up his elbow to ward off the blow.

William turned and ran as fast as he could back to the village. By good luck a policeman was standing outside the general shop, idly examining a row of dusty birthday cards that had been there for the past eighteen months.

'Come quick!' gasped William. 'Miss Smith's soldier's killin' the tramp.'

The policeman turned and stared at him.

'*Killin'* him, I tell you,' repeated William. 'Come on quick or you'll be too late.'

'None of your tricks, now,' said the policeman, but there was something convincing about William's excitement, and, in any case, he was tired of the birthday cards . . . He accompanied William across the field to the old barn.

'Go on! Look through the crack,' urged William.

But this was, apparently, inconsistent with the dignity of the policeman. Instead, he put his shoulder to the large but insecure door and shoved it open. The scene it revealed was different from the one William had watched through the crack. The soldier was still standing over the tramp in a threatening attitude, but Miss Smith was now crouching on the ground in an attitude of distress. To William, it looked like a hastily-assumed attitude of distress, but he realised that to the policeman, seeing it for the first time, it must appear real enough. The soldier turned to the policeman. He was Miss Smith's soldier again – courteous, gentle, if a little stern.

'I'm glad you've come, officer,' he said. 'I found this brute assaulting Miss Smith. I heard her cries for help as I

MISS SMITH WAS CROUCHING IN AN ATTITUDE OF
DISTRESS.

came up the field and I've been giving him a little of what
he deserved.'

'I ain't done nuffin', guv'ner,' whined the tramp. He
shuffled to his feet and came into the light, revealing a
black eye and a bleeding nose. 'I ain't done nuffin' an' look
'ow 'e's knocked me abaht . . .'

'You brute!' sobbed Miss Smith.

The policeman laid an ungentle hand on the tramp's
shoulder.

'You come along with me,' he said sternly, and then,
respectfully, to Miss Smith's soldier: 'If you'll just give me

the particulars, sir . . .' He took out note-book and pencil. 'You say you found this man assaulting Miss Smith?'

'Yes. Assaulting Miss Smith.'

The policeman began to write slowly and laboriously. 'Ass-aulting . . . How many s's, sir?'

'Two.'

'I gone and put three.'

He began to hunt in his pocket. William suddenly remembered his newly acquired rubber and brought it out proudly, wiping the crumbs from it.

'Here's a rubber,' he said.

The policeman took it, rubbed the offending s, then scowled suspiciously at William.

'None of your tricks!' he said. 'This ain't no rubber. It don't rub, anyway.'

'I thought it was,' said William apologetically. 'I found it in a tea-cake.'

Then, for the first time, he noticed Miss Smith and her soldier. Their eyes were fixed in frozen horror on the rubber. Their faces had turned a greenish white. The policeman was still examining the rubber.

'Seems to have a sort of cap on,' he said.

He took the cap off and pulled out a small roll of paper. Then the strangest event of the whole afternoon happened. For the tramp was no longer a tramp, except in

257

THE TRAMP SPRANG AT MISS SMITH'S SOLDIER.

appearance. He sprang at Miss Smith's soldier and pinned him in an expert grip from behind.

'Get the woman, Constable,' he said. 'Don't let her go, whatever you do . . . And you,' to William, 'cut down to the police station and tell them to send a car at once. My name's Finch. They know me . . .'

The policeman was no less bewildered than William, but he recognised the voice of Authority when he heard it and sprang to Miss Smith, who fought and bit and scratched with unexpected ferocity before she was finally mastered. William, also recognising the voice of Authority, cut down to the police station . . .

It turned out the Fräulein Schmitt did not, after all, love the 'country of her adoption'. She was, in fact, a fanatical Nazi agent who had come over among the refugees in order to carry on the work of espionage. Her soldier had not fought in the last war or in any other war. He was not even lame. He was the son of German parents who, though naturalised, had worked for the 'Fatherland' ever since they came to England. It turned out that Miss Smith, hovering attentively over the airmen at the canteen while they ate their scrambled eggs or beans on toast, picked up a good many items of news that were of interest to the Führer's representatives. These, together with other items that she picked up from the conversation of the officers who came to tea or dinner at the Vicarage, were carefully recorded in code, packed into a small asbestos container, in shape resembling a rubber, and baked into the 'tea-cake' for which her 'soldier' called each week. Authority had for some time suspected Fräulein Schmitt of pro-enemy activity but could prove nothing. She wrote no letters and received no letters. She never left the neighbourhood and seemed to have no friends among the other refugees. It was Mrs Mason's article that had first given Mr Finch (of what is known as the Secret Service) the idea. There might be nothing in this tea-cake business, of course, but it was worth investigating. A stranger visiting the village would have caused comment and put Fräulein Schmitt on her guard. An old tramp, wandering through the village and cadging food at the canteen, would rouse no interest. He was lucky, of course, to find William there . . .

'Why didn't you biff him one while he was knocking you about?' asked William when he heard the story. 'I bet you could have done.'

Mr Finch grinned.

'I could have done, my boy, and, I can tell you, I wanted to, but I hadn't got hold of anything.'

'You mean you hadn't got a clue?' said William, remembering his detective stories.

'I mean I hadn't got a clue,' said Mr Finch. 'I felt that, if I held on, something might slip out that would give it to me.'

'I gave it you,' said William proudly.

'You did, my boy, and I'm grateful to you . . . Good thing the bobby couldn't spell, eh?'

The news had already sped round the village. William walked homewards with a rollicking swagger. He would be famous now, he thought, for the rest of his life . . . But he was too late. Already Mrs Mason was typing her latest article: 'How I Trapped a German Spy'.

CHAPTER 10

THE BATTLE OF FLOWERS

'WE'VE gotter get somethin' ready for Vict'ry,' said William. 'Everyone else is doin' somethin'.'

'What sort of thing?' demanded Ginger.

'Some people are gettin' up Vict'ry balls . . .' said Henry.

'We jolly well don't want a Vict'ry ball. Dancin' with rotten ole girls! We get enough of that at the dancin' class. I never have seen what people see in it, dancin'.'

'They're gettin' up a pageant where my aunt lives,' said Douglas. 'She's goin' to be Queen Elizabeth.'

'I thouldn't mind bein' her,' said Violet Elizabeth graciously. 'It wath only 'cauth of mumpth I wathn't her before.'

'You won't be in it at all,' said William sternly. 'No one asked you to the meetin' anyway.'

'If Joan can come, why thouldn't I?' demanded Violet Elizabeth.

''Cause we asked Joan. She helps. You only mess everything up.'

Violet Elizabeth looked at Joan who sat, small and shy

261

and earnest, on an upturned packing case in a corner of the old barn.

'Thee's got thoot on her nothe,' she remarked dispassionately.

Joan took out her handkerchief and rubbed off the infinitesimal speck.

'We had the chimney sweep this morning,' she explained.

'You leave her alone,' said William indignantly to Violet Elizabeth.

'I only thaid thee had thoot on her nothe,' said Violet Elizabeth with devastating sweetness. 'I thought thee'd like to know. I'd like to know if I had thoot on my nothe. Anyway' – she smiled on them serenely – 'you can't turn me out. If you try I'll thcream an' thcream an' *thcream*.'

William sighed, deciding for the hundredth time that girls complicated every situation into which one admitted them. Joan was a different matter. She lacked the ruthlessness and dominating personality of Violet Elizabeth. She was quiet and amenable and willing to help. She joined the Outlaws as a slave. Violet Elizabeth, despite the disarming camouflage of meekness that she could assume for her own ends, joined it as a tyrant.

'Well, we aren't havin' any girls in whatever we do for this Vict'ry show,' said William.

He spoke firmly, but there was something in the curve of Violet Elizabeth's cherubic lips and in the light of her wide blue eyes that made him feel a good deal less confident than he sounded.

'You can help if you want,' he added, 'but that's jolly well all.'

'That'th all we want to do, ithn't it, Joan?' said Violet Elizabeth.

'Yes,' agreed Joan earnestly.

'What do they *do* in pageants?' asked William.

'They sort of act things out of hist'ry,' said Henry.

'You'll have to have girlth if ith hithtory, William,' said Violet Elizabeth with quiet satisfaction. 'Hithtory'th full of them – queenth and thingth.'

'They sort of act without talkin',' said Henry, ignoring her.

'How do people know what they're actin' if they don't talk?' said William.

'They've jus' gotter guess, I s'pose,' said Henry.

'I see,' said William thoughtfully. 'If a man comes on in a crown, wearin' a rose, it'd be Charles I in the Wars of the Roses, or somethin' like that.'

'Yes, somethin' like that,' agreed Henry doubtfully, 'but I don't think it was Charles I in the Wars of the Roses.'

'Well, Charles II, then,' said William impatiently. 'An' if someone comes on an' puts a coat over a puddle it'd be that man who put his coat down for Queen Elizabeth. The Black Prince, wasn't it?'

'Sir Walter Raleigh,' murmured Henry.

'Yes, I knew it was either him or the Black Prince,' said William.

'I thaid you'd have to have girlth,' said Violet Elizabeth with a radiant smile. 'I *thaid* tho.'

'Well, we're not goin' to,' said William. 'I bet I could do Queen Elizabeth all right.'

'I'm sure you could,' said Joan, but Violet Elizabeth burst into a peal of silvery laughter.

'I'd love to thee you,' she said. 'You'd look tho funny.'

'Anyway, we're not doin' that,' said William irritably. 'We're not goin' to copy anyone. We're goin' to think out somethin' of our own.'

'Sometimes they have someone readin' aloud in po'try what they're actin' while they're actin' it,' said Henry, reluctant to leave a subject on which he felt himself to be an authority.

'Well, we're not goin' to have anythin' out of hist'ry,' said William firmly. 'We get enough of that in school. All that fuss las' week jus' cause I said that ole Caxton invented the steam engine 'stead of Wat Tyler or whoever it was!' Henry opened his mouth to protest then closed it again as William continued: 'Anyway, what does it matter what they're called? It's jus' a name their mother happened to think of an' she might jus' as well have thought of somethin' else. I bet she'd have called him Wat Tyler, or whatever it was, if she'd thought of it. I've got an aunt that always calls me Robert an' Robert William an' no one tells her that she's a monument of c'lossal ignorance an' crass stupidity an' all the things ole Markie called me. What does it matter what people's names are, anyway?'

He paused for breath, and Ginger said mildly:

'Well, we aren't any nearer findin' what to do for this Vict'ry show.'

'No, but we can jolly well keep off history,' said William, in a voice that still held the aftermath of bitterness.

'If it's a Vict'ry show,' said Joan, 'let's have somethin' about Vict'ry.'

'That's a good idea,' said William, impressed.

'I wath juth going to thuggetht it,' said Violet Elizabeth serenely.

'We could have Britannia,' said Joan, 'riding in a sort of chariot. A wheelbarrow would do. Or that box on wheels you've got.'

'I'll be Britannia,' said Violet Elizabeth. 'My mother'th got a Britannia fanthy-dreth cothtume.'

'You jolly well won't,' said William. 'If we have girls in it at all, Joan's being Britannia.'

'Thee can't be,' said Violet Elizabeth. 'Thee hathn't got a Britannia fanthy-dreth cothtume.'

'You could lend her yours, couldn't you?'

'Yeth,' said Violet Elizabeth, still smiling serenely. 'But I won't . . .'

'Then you're a rotten mean ole girl.'

'And after Britannia we could have some British soldiers,' said Joan, hastily intervening before the quarrel could reach such proportions as to hold up progress indefinitely. 'We could easily get some boys to be those. And then we could have Germany and captured German prisoners.'

'Who'd be them?' said Douglas doubtfully. 'I bet no one'd want to be them.'

'We could fix that up later,' said William. 'It's a jolly good idea, anyway.' He turned to Violet Elizabeth. 'Would you like to be Germany? It's a jolly good part.'

'What thould I wear?' said Violet Elizabeth. 'It dependth on what I'd wear.'

They considered the question.

'Swashtikas,' suggested Henry.

'No,' said Violet Elizabeth firmly. 'I don't like thwath-tikath!'

'Sackcloth,' said Ginger.

'No,' said Violet Elizabeth, still more firmly. 'I don't like thackcloth.' Suddenly her small face beamed. '*Tell* you what! I've got a fanthy dreth at home I could wear. Ith a fanthy dreth of a rothe. Ith got a thkirt of pink thilk petalth, all thtanding out, and pink thilk thtockingth and thoeth. And ith got a pink rothe-bud for a cap. A couthin of mine had it before the war and thee sent it to me 'cauth thee'd grown out of it and it would juth fit me now. I wouldn't mind being Germany if I could wear that.'

'Well, you can't,' said William shortly.

'But, William, ith a *pretty* dreth,' she assured him earnestly. 'You could thow a thwathika on if you like,' she conceded. 'Thomewhere where it wouldn't thow.'

'If you think——' began William portentously, but she interrupted him.

'And I muth ride in the chariot and I muth go on firtht in front of Britannia.'

She smiled at them radiantly, as if she had completely solved the problem.

'You can't do that if you're Germany,' said William.

'Why not?'

''Cause – 'cause you've gotter be sorry for all the wrong you've done.'

'Well, I'm not,' said Violet Elizabeth with spirit, 'and I haven't done any wrong.'

'You started the war.'

'I didn't,' snapped Violet Elizabeth. 'I wath in bed with a billiouth attack the day the war thtarted. Athk the doctor if you don't believe me.'

'You're bats,' said William. 'It's no good talking to you. An' we jolly well don't want you in the show anyway.'

'Then you can't have the Britannia cothtume.'

'We don't want it,' said William untruthfully.

'I don't mind Violet Elizabeth being Britannia,' said Joan, anxious that the success of the pageant should not be jeopardised by jealousy among the cast.

'Well, we do,' said William. He turned to Violet Elizabeth. 'You're not going to be in it, so you can clear off. We've got a lot of things to discuss.'

'I'll thtay and lithen to you dithcuthing them,' said Violet Elizabeth, with the air of one granting a favour.

'People with manners,' said William crushingly, 'don't stay where they're not wanted.'

'I'm not a perthon with mannerth,' said Violet Elizabeth, uncrushed, 'and I like thtaying where I'm not wanted. It'th gen'rally more interethting than where I am wanted.'

'We'll carry on as if she wasn't there,' said William to the others. 'She's just not worth taking any notice of. I'm glad she's not going to be in it. She's always more bother than she's worth.'

He could not help glancing at Violet Elizabeth as he spoke, hoping to see her look conscience-stricken or at least abashed, but she met his glance with a smile of shattering sweetness.

'Well, now,' he went on hastily. 'We've got a lot to arrange. Joan'll be Britannia, and we can easily fix up a costume for her with flags and things an' she'll come on in this cart, drawn by two of us, an' we'll write some po'try for someone to say when she comes on. Who can write po'try?' He looked round the circle, carefully avoiding Violet Elizabeth's eye.

'I can thay *Cargoeth*,' said Violet Elizabeth proudly.

They ignored her.

'You can, can't you, Joan?' said William.

'I can try,' said Joan doubtfully. 'I once wrote a poem about a mouse.'

'Thay it,' challenged Violet Elizabeth.

Again they ignored her.

'Then we'll get some boys to be soldiers,' said William. 'Marchin' an' drillin' and so on . . .'

'I don't thee what mithe have got to do with a Victory pageant,' said Violet Elizabeth.

'Nobody asked you,' said William. 'I wish you'd shut up.'

'All right,' said Violet Elizabeth, with unexpected

meekness. 'I only thought it was thilly thaying po'try about mithe at a Victory pageant and it *ith*.'

'Well, let's get on with things,' said William. There was no doubt that Violet Elizabeth's interruptions had a disintegrating effect on the discussion. It was difficult to pick up the threads again. 'After these soldiers, we'll have Germany. I bet we'll get a jolly good Germany an' we'll get a jolly good dress for whoever it is, too, with sackcloth and swastikas and things.'

'It'th *thuth* a pretty pink thilk dreth, William,' said Violet Elizabeth wistfully. 'It'th got little pearl beadth thewn on for dew dropth. I don't know why you won't let me wear it.'

'Well, we won't,' said William testily. 'We only want you to shut up.' He turned to the others. 'Then, after Germany, we'll have the captured German prisoners . . . I *say*! Couldn't we get Hubert Lane and his gang to be the captured German prisoners?'

The Outlaws thought of the Hubert Laneites, between whom and the Outlaws a feud had existed as long as any of them could remember.

'They'd make jolly good German prisoners,' agreed Ginger, 'but I bet they wouldn't do it.'

'Couldn't we capture them?'

'If we did, we couldn't keep them till the pageant.'

'Let's ask them to do it. Let's make out that it's the most important part. They're jolly stupid.'

'Yes, but they're not quite as stupid as that.'

'Where shall we have it, anyway? Where do people have pageants?'

'They generally have them in the grounds of castles or big houses,' said Henry.

'Our houthe ith the only big houthe in the village,' said Violet Elizabeth triumphantly, 'an' I won't let you have it in our garden unleth you let me be Britannia and wear my pink thilk dreth, tho there! I don't thuppothe,' she added thoughtfully, 'that my mother would let you have it there, anyway, 'cauthe thee doethn't like you. Thee thayth that you're rough, an' rude, an' badly behaved, and you *are,* and I'm going home now, and you'll be *thorry* one day that you've been tho nathty to me.'

Thereupon, Violet Elizabeth withdrew with an impressive air of dignity which did not quite desert her even when she turned at the door and put out her tongue at them.

'Well, thank goodness she's gone!' said William. 'Now we can get on with things a bit.'

But their project was still beset with difficulties – Germany, the German prisoners, the scene of the pageant . . .

'We can't have it at the Hall now Violet Elizabeth's not in it.'

'There's the Manor at Marleigh,' said Joan.

'They wouldn't let us have it there.'

'They're away. I heard my mother saying that Sir Gerald and Lady Markham had shut up the Manor and gone to Scotland. And they've let nearly all the garden to a market gardener at Marleigh. They've only kept the lawn and the part just outside the house and one old gardener.'

'That sounds all right,' said William, brightening. 'An' I bet they won't be there for Vict'ry. They'll go to London for it. High-up people do. I bet he'll be carryin' a banner or holdin' a sceptre or somethin' in the procession. An' I know that ole gardener. He's got an arm-chair in the greenhouse, an' he does his Football Pools there all day, an' he's deaf an' nearly blind, an' never takes any notice of anythin'. He'd probably think we'd got permission . . .'

This was felt to be a little over-optimistic, but it seemed to be the best plan in the circumstances.

'We'll rehearse ordin'ry in the old barn,' said William, 'but we'll have the dress rehearsal an' the real show at the Manor. You'll start writin' your po'try, won't you, Joan?' and, with a somewhat confused memory of Violet Elizabeth's strictures, added: 'It needn't be about mice, you know.'

'Of course not,' said Joan, a little irritably. 'I only said I once wrote a poem about a mouse.'

'An' we'll get some boys for soldiers, an'' – not very hopefully – 'I'll try an' fix up with the Hubert Laneites to be German prisoners.'

He approached Hubert Lane the next day.

'Say, Hubert,' he said. 'We're goin' to get up a sort of Vict'ry pageant.'

Hubert's fat face spread into a grin.

'Yeah?' he said.

There seemed to be something more offensive than usual in the grin, but William ignored it.

'I wonder whether you an' your gang'd like parts in it?'

Again Hubert said: 'Yeah?'

'They're the best parts in the show,' said William. 'We thought it wasn't worth offerin' you anythin' but the best parts. We don't mind takin' the worst parts ourselves 'cause we're gettin' it up an' we don't want the best parts. We want you to have 'em.'

'Kind of you,' said Hubert, with a sneer, but the sneer was so much his usual expression that, again, William ignored it.

'Well?' he said.

'What parts are they?' said Hubert.

'Jolly important ones,' said William. 'They're – they're German prisoners.'

'Funny, that,' said Hubert ruminatively.

'What?'

'I was jus' goin' to ask you an' your gang to be German prisoners in our pageant.'

'Your pageant?' said William.

'Yeah,' said Hubert, with an intensification of his sneer. 'We're gettin' up a Vict'ry pageant. Violet Elizabeth's goin' to be Britannia – her mother's got a jolly good Britannia costume – an' we're goin' to be British soldiers, an' we're goin' to get someone to be Germany, an' we were goin' to ask you to be German prisoners. All you'd need would be a rope tied round your necks . . .'

William stared at him, speechless with horror. He had not thought even Violet Elizabeth capable of such depths of perfidy . . .

'Violet Elizabeth's goin' to make up some po'try about it,' continued Hubert suavely. 'It ought to be a jolly good pageant. Mrs Bott's goin' to let us do it on the lawn at the Hall, an' all the children in the village have promised to come. We're goin' to give 'em tea . . . Well, what about it? Will you be German prisoners? You'd make jolly good German prisoners.'

Then, seeing the light of battle in William's eye, he took to flight. William pursued him half-heartedly for a few yards, then returned to break the news to the others.

'She's pinched our pageant an' she's gettin' it up with the Hubert Laneites,' he announced. 'Would anyone have thought she'd be as mean as that?'

'Yes, I would,' said Joan simply.

'What are we goin' to do?' said Ginger.

'We're goin' on with it,' said William firmly. 'We're not goin' to give it up jus' for a mean ole girl like that. *Gosh!* Would you have thought it? Jus' because she couldn't be Britannia! Sickening! I bet even Hitler wouldn't have done a thing like that.'

So, doggedly, they continued their preparations for their pageant, but somehow the zest had gone out of it. It wasn't only the fact of the rival pageant that was being organised and rehearsed in the grounds of the Hall under Violet Elizabeth's despotic rule. It was the absence of Violet Elizabeth herself. They had resented her presence among them and heartily wished her away but, now that she had gone, they missed her – missed her dynamic personality, her unreasonableness, her contrariness, her varying moods, her uncertain temper, even her lisp . . . Their loyalty to Joan was unchanged, but she was almost too docile and amenable and ready to fall in with their suggestions. She failed to provide the stimulus that Violet Elizabeth had always provided. And, though they would not have admitted it, they felt wounded and betrayed.

That Violet Elizabeth, their most troublesome but most loyal follower, should have joined the Hubert Laneites was almost too monstrous for belief.

Joan did her best. She wrote her 'poetry' with frowning concentration, sucking her pencil to induce inspiration and drawing it across her forehead in moments of deep thought till her brow resembled a complicated railway map. For the Britannia costume she had decided to stitch flags on to her white frock, but she had not yet been able to obtain any flags. Everyone who had them was keeping them for their own Victory decorations and the village shop was sold out.

'I'm sure to get some before the day,' she said. 'I expect there'll be heaps in the shop by then.'

William concentrated his efforts on drilling his band of soldiers. He had found no difficulty in obtaining recruits. The only difficulty was in organising them. They were apt to scuffle and scrimmage and indulge in horseplay highly unsuitable to British soldiers in a Victory parade. The rehearsals offered an excellent opportunity of paying off private scores and generally ended in a free fight in which everyone joined just for the fun of the thing whether he had any private scores to pay off or not. William tried to divide them into groups of soldiers, sailors, airmen, Commandos and paratroops, but the free fight would break out again immediately and the ranks would become inextricably mingled.

'You can't go on like this,' he said despairingly, 'fightin' all the time.'

'That's what soldiers are for, isn't it?' they replied.

'They're for fightin' an enemy, not each other,' said William.

'Give us an enemy, then.'

'I tried to,' said William. 'I tried to get the Hubert Laneites, but they wouldn't come.'

The Hubert Laneites were keeping well out of the Outlaws' way, while carrying on energetic preparations for their own pageant. The Outlaws watched them from the road through the hedge, as Violet Elizabeth rehearsed them ruthlessly in the garden of the Hall.

'Gosh! She's puttin' 'em through it,' said William. 'Thank goodness it's them, not us, now!'

'Thank goodness!' echoed the Outlaws with relief that did not ring quite true.

Once they met Violet Elizabeth in the road outside the Hall. She passed them without looking at them, head in air. They passed her in silence, refraining by tacit consent from jeers or hostilities. Her treachery went too deep for that . . .

They gathered that the Hubert Laneites, like themselves, had been unable to persuade anyone to take the parts of Germany or of the German prisoners. Otherwise their preparations were on a lavish scale. Mrs Bott had promised cakes, lemonade and ice cream..

'I don't see what good it is, goin' on with the thing at all,' said Ginger gloomily. 'No one'll come to it, anyway, with the Hubert Laneites havin' it at the Hall on the same day an' givin' them tea.'

'I'm not goin' to stop it 'cause of *them*,' said William firmly. 'I'm jolly well goin' on with it, whether anyone comes or not.'

A reconnoitring expedition to Marleigh Manor proved on the whole satisfactory. It was empty and deserted. The front lawn slept peacefully in the sunshine. The gardener slept peacefully in the greenhouse. Trees screened the lawn from observation on all sides except the house.

'It's a jolly good place for it,' said William. 'We'll have the dress rehearsal as soon as we've got it ready.'

The dress rehearsal was fixed for the next Saturday, and the cast assembled in the old barn early in the afternoon. Joan had tried up to the last minute to obtain some flags but without success, and had had to content herself with pinning a red, white and blue rosette and a Royal Engineers' badge on her white frock and putting a green silk tea cosy on her head. She carried a toasting fork for a trident and the costume was considered by the others to be an adequate, if not striking, representation of Britannia. William, as Commander-in-Chief, wore a tin hat and his father's Home Guard boots. The others, who had been told to collect 'uniforms' from whatever sources they could, presented a motley spectacle. One wore a fancy-dress costume of Robin Hood and carried a poker. Another wore a very ancient fancy-dress costume of Henry the Fifth, the coat of mail knitted in dishcloth cotton from which the aluminium paint had long since disappeared, and from which dangled several tempting odds and ends of dishcloth cotton. Another wore a red Indian costume with feathered head-dress. Another, who had once taken part in a charade as an Ancient Briton, wore a fur rug, with a tray for a shield. One wore a gas mask, another a saucepan, another a fire guard . . .

Putting an end, as well as he could, to the inevitable skirmish, William addressed them in his most impressive manner.

'Now look here,' he said. 'Stop messin' about an' listen to me. We're goin' over to Marleigh Manor for the dress rehearsal an' – stop bangin' your tray, Victor Jameson – an' we'll go by the fields an' keep by the hedge 'cause we don't want a lot of people seein' us – stop blowin' that trumpet,

George Bell – an' we'll go on to the lawn through the shrub'ry from the road an' do it under the tree at the end of the lawn same as we said – stop pullin' the fur out of his rug, Ginger. He told you it'd got the moth in – an' I bet it'll be all right with it bein' Sat'day. That ole gardener always takes Sat'day off, so we can go right through the pageant without bein' int'rupted. Stop unwinding his coat of mail, Freddie Parker. I don't care if you are windin' it into a nice ball. What's he goin' to do with only about an inch of coat of mail left? Now get into line – Joan first, then me, then the rest of you – an' don't make so much noise. We don't want everyone knowin' about it before the day.'

It had been decided to dispense with the chariot for the dress rehearsal, so Joan, looking solemn and intense in her white dress and green tea cosy, the exercise book containing her 'poetry' under her arm, set off at the head of the procession. William followed, leading his motley band of warriors, still scuffling and scrimmaging but in a more subdued manner.

They climbed the hill to Marleigh by way of the fields, keeping to the shadow of the hedge, as William had directed, and attracting no attention except from an old horse, who gazed at them with an expression of incredulous amazement and then uttered a neigh that sounded like a burst of derisive laughter.

'Shut up!' said William. 'You look a jolly sight funnier than we do, anyway.'

They made their way through the shrubbery and on to the front lawn of Marleigh Manor.

And there they had their first shock.

For the lawn was full of children – bored, listless-looking children – sitting in serried rows facing the empty space under the copper beech where William had planned to hold his pageant. For a few moments he was much too taken aback to do anything but stare at them; then, reacting automatically to the situation, he led his band on to the open space and started proceedings.

'Ladies an' gentlemen,' he began. 'This is our Vict'ry pageant, an' this is Joan – I mean Britannia. Go on, Joan.'

Joan opened her book, glanced at it for a moment or two to refresh her memory, and began her recital.

'I am Britannia, ruling the waves
And Britons that never, never, never,
Never shall be slaves.'

She stood aside and motioned forward the motley band of warriors.

'These are British soldiers that won the war

And aren't going to fight any more.
Soldiers on land and sailors on the seas
And Commandos jumping down from trees,
And paratroops coming down from the skies,
And now the war's over it's going to be very nice.'

Here each branch of the services, as drilled by
William, was to have given a display of its particular
activity. The soldiers were to march and make a show of
shooting with imaginary rifles, the sailors to scan the
horizon with imaginary telescopes, Commandos and
paratroops to swarm up the copper beech and drop
lightly from its branches. This had never yet gone
according to plan, and it was obvious that it was not
going to do so today. In fact, the usual scrimmage was
just in process of forming itself, when—

The Outlaws received their second shock.

For Violet Elizabeth, dressed in her pink silk rose costume, appeared at the head of the Hubert Laneites and led
them up to William, smiling radiantly.

'I wath only teathing you, William,' she said. 'I've got
a lovely thurprithe for you.'

She turned the radiant smile on to the audience and,
striking an attitude, proclaimed:

'I am ole Germany, Beat in the war,
A goothe that won't go goothe-thtepping any more.'

She pointed to Hubert, who wore a row of medals on his coat.

'Here'th ole Goering,
He ithn't purring
Any more.'

She next pointed to Bertie Franks, who had a short moustache corked upon his upper lip.

'Here'th the ole Führer.
He won't go to Nürnberg any more.'

Next she waved her hand airily to Claude Bellew, a thin, undersized member of Hubert's gang.

'Here'th ole Goebbleth the liar.
He won't say London's on fire
Any more.'

A wave of both hands included the rest of the Hubert Laneites.

'I'VE GOT A LOVELY THURPRITHE FOR YOU, WILLIAM,' SAID
VIOLET ELIZABETH.

'And here'th the ole German prithonerth,
Their generalth, too,
Looking juth like the monkeyth
You thee in the zoo.'

The Hubert Laneites stared at her, speechless with
fury, aghast at the trick that had been played on them.

For Violet Elizabeth had joined them, offering to
organise their pageant, act the part of Britannia, and even
help them capture the Outlaws for German prisoners. She
had cast Hubert Lane for the part of Churchill, stipulat-
ing that he must have a row of medals, which, she assured
him, Churchill always wore. So Hubert, who was rather
stupid, procured the medals. She had assigned to Bertie
Franks the part of Mr Eden and had corked his moustache
herself, assuring him that the likeness was now so perfect
that no one could tell the difference. Claude Bellew, she
had said, must be Monty, Georgie Parker and the rest of
them British soldiers. Instead of which, she had shame-
lessly delivered them into the hands of their enemies,
making them play the hateful and humiliating part themselves in the Outlaws' pageant.

She stood there, smiling proudly.

'Ithn't it a lovely thurprithe, William?' she said.

The infuriated Hubert Laneites flung themselves upon

the Outlaws. The Outlaws flung themselves upon the Hubert Laneites. The battle spread to the audience, and the audience, losing its air of listlessness, flung itself upon both sides impartially.

Struggling masses of children surged to and fro over the lawn. Hubert Lane dodged round the summer house with William in hot pursuit. A member of the audience had got Bertie Franks down on the ground and was filling his mouth with grass. Claude Bellew was half-way up the copper beech with Ginger hanging on to his leg and trying to pull him down. Henry the Fifth was wrestling with his own disintegrating costume, his ankles pinioned by yards of tangled dishcloth cotton. The peaceful summer air was rent by shouts and yells and war-whoops.

Then a sudden silence fell.

Lady Markham was making her way to them over the lawn from the house.

And here the Outlaws got their third shock.

For she was smiling in unmistakable welcome. She held out her hand to William and clasped his warmly.

'Thank you, my dear boy,' she said. '*Thank* you.'

Every summer Sir Gerald and Lady Markham invited a party of slum children to spend an afternoon in the grounds and partake of a tea that had continued even in wartime to be comparatively lavish. They were a conscientious couple, deeply sensible of their obligations to the community in general and, though they had closed the Manor and were spending the summer in Scotland, they decided to come back for the usual Saturday of the children's visit and do the thing in style, as they had always done. They had prepared the lavish tea. They had engaged a conjuror to do conjuring tricks on the lawn. They had engaged a Punch and Judy show to follow. And then, when the audience had arrived – shy and ill-at-ease and even slightly resentful, as it generally was at first – the conjuror rang up to say that he had sprained his ankle, and a few minutes later the Punch and Judy man rang up to say that he was down with 'flu. Lady Markham telephoned every entertainment agency she knew. No one was free on such short notice. Frantically she rang up all her friends. None of them had any suggestions except one who offered to recite passages from Shakespeare, and another who offered to give a lecture on 'Home Life in the Eighteenth Century' which she had given at the Women's Institute the week before and which had, she said, been well received by the few who had turned up to listen to it. Meantime the audience sat, bored and impassive, waiting . . .

And then the miracle had happened.

'I don't know who sent the children,' said Lady Markham afterwards. 'Or whether it was their own idea.

They must, of course, have heard of the dilemma I was in, because I'd simply rung up everyone I knew to tell them about it. I was feeling simply *desperate,* when I looked out of the window and saw these children coming to my rescue. It really was a charming idea. A children's Battle of Flowers. First came a little girl dressed as a snowdrop, followed by her pages, then came a little girl dressed as a rose, followed by her pages. The pages, of course, were rather strangely dressed, but, considering the war and everything, it was excellent. Then they started this Battle of the Flowers and invited the audience to join in, and then the whole thing went like a house on fire. It became just a little bit rough, I admit, but the children enjoyed it and that was the chief thing.'

'Splendid effort, my boy,' said Sir Gerald, grasping William's hand in his turn. 'Simply splendid! I can't tell you how grateful my wife and I are to you . . . Ice broken all right now, eh?'

The ice was certainly broken, together with most of the chairs and benches on which the audience had been sitting, but host and hostess gazed at the chaos with smiles of unalloyed pleasure.

'Such a relief!' said Lady Markham. 'These afternoons have always been a success. I should have been miserable if this one had been a failure. You and your friends will stay to tea, won't you, and help us till the little visitors go?'

Dazedly William promised that he would. Dazedly he returned to the fray. The Battle of Flowers had developed into a game which everyone played according to his own rules, and in which everyone seemed to know what he was doing, though no one else did. The little visitors leapt and screamed and shouted and pushed.

'It's the best party we've ever 'ad here,' said one of them to William. 'I'm jolly glad they asked you.'

They clustered round the trestle tables in the hall, dishevelled and panting, and began the attack upon jellies, sandwiches, cakes, buns. Sir Gerald and Lady Markham hovered gratefully about William, pressing delicacies upon him.

'It really is good of you, you know,' said Sir Gerald, 'giving up your Saturday afternoon to getting us out of a hole like this.'

William grinned sheepishly and took another slab of chocolate cake.

*

Violet Elizabeth and Joan stood on one side and watched proceedings with an air of aloofness, daintily nibbling chocolate biscuits.

'It's a very pretty frock,' said Joan generously.

'Yourth ith pretty, too,' said Violet Elizabeth, not to be outdone in generosity, and added: 'An' yourth wath a very nithe piethe of poetry.'

'You didn't make up that poetry yourself, did you?' said Joan.

'No,' admitted Violet Elizabeth, with what on any less angelic face would have been a grin. 'I got my couthin to do it. Thee'th clever.'

They watched the boys scuffling round the table, wolfing the lavish tea.

'Jutht look at them,' said Violet Elizabeth, elevating her small nose. 'Aren't they dithguthting?'

'They haven't any manners, boys,' said Joan.

The two felt themselves to be withdrawn into a rarified atmosphere of feminine superiority.

'They haven't any mannerth and they haven't any thenth,' said Violet Elizabeth severely. 'I thay, will you come to tea at our houthe tomorrow, and we won't have any boyth?'

'Yes, I'd like to,' said Joan.

William approached them, his mouth still full of chocolate cake.

'We're goin' out to play rounders,' he said indistinctly. 'Come on.'

Violet Elizabeth looked at him disdainfully.

'What a meth you're in!' she said, with an odious imitation of grown-up disapproval. 'Joan and I don't care for thothe childith gameth. We're going to walk round the garden, aren't we, Joan?'

'Yes,' said Joan.

They walked off, arm in arm, without looking back.

William stood staring after them, baffled and crestfallen, pondering on the incomprehensibility of the female sex. Then he shrugged his shoulders, dismissed the problem, and ran to join the riot on the lawn . . .

A selected list of titles available from Macmillan Children's Books

The prices shown below are correct at the time of going to press. However, Macmillan Publishers reserves the right to show new retail prices on covers, which may differ from those previously advertised.

Richmal Crompton

Just William	978-0-330-53534-2	£5.99
More William	978-0-330-53535-9	£5.99
William Again	978-0-330-54518-1	£5.99
William the Fourth	978-0-330-54517-4	£5.99
Still William	978-0-330-54470-2	£5.99
William the Conqueror	978-0-330-54519-8	£5.99
William the Outlaw	978-0-330-54524-2	£5.99
William in Trouble	978-0-330-54471-9	£5.99
William the Good	978-0-330-54525-9	£5.99

All Pan Macmillan titles can be ordered from our website, www.panmacmillan.com, or from your local bookshop and are also available by post from:

Bookpost, PO Box 29, Douglas, Isle of Man IM99 1BQ

Credit cards accepted. For details:
Telephone: 01624 677237
Fax: 01624 670923
Email: bookshop@enterprise.net
www.bookpost.co.uk

Free postage and packing in the United Kingdom